NO ONE WILL EVER KNOW

ENDORSEMENTS

"Once I started reading this book, I couldn't put it down. I love the way the author connects the dots between our modern-day problems and God's warnings to us passed down through many centuries of Scripture."

—VALORIE MCNEILL SMITH
Christian vet tech, retired

"I know many people who need to read this book and apply it to their lives."

—DEBBIE OLINGER
Christian Parks and Recreation facilities manager

"This book is relatable on a personal level and perfectly illustrates God's love, mercy, and grace, which He extends to all of us—all we have to do is ask."

—NIKOLE PENNINGTON
Christian waitress

"The author leads his readers toward valuable lessons in taking responsibility, showing compassion, and, most of all, seeking and giving forgiveness by following the wisdom of God's Word."

—LEANNE GAMM
Christian Physical Therapist Assistant

NO ONE WILL EVER KNOW

C. M. NEEDHAM

AMBASSADOR INTERNATIONAL
GREENVILLE, SOUTH CAROLINA & BELFAST, NORTHERN IRELAND
www.ambassador-international.com

NO ONE WILL EVER KNOW

©2025 by C. M. Needham
All rights reserved

ISBN: 978-1-64960-427-9
eISBN: 978-1-64960-475-0

Cover Design by Karen Slayne
Interior Typesetting by Dentelle Design
Edited by Emily Caseres

Scripture quotations taken from the King James Version of the Bible. Public Domain.

AMBASSADOR INTERNATIONAL
Emerald House
411 University Ridge, Suite B14
Greenville, SC 29601
United States
www.ambassador-international.com

AMBASSADOR BOOKS
The Mount
2 Woodstock Link
Belfast, BT6 8DD
Northern Ireland, United Kingdom
www.ambassadormedia.co.uk

The colophon is a trademark of Ambassador, a Christian publishing company.

For Dixie,

resting peacefully in the loving arms of Jesus

"The fool hath said in his heart, there is no God."

Psalm 14:1

PREFACE

This is a work of fiction into which biblical truth is woven. Characters and situations are fabrications taken from events I've witnessed through my seventy plus years of life.

In the early 1980s, I met Dixie, a Christian woman who became a dear friend. From time to time, she received visions from the throne room. One of her visions involved me. In that vision, she said she saw a young woman crying as she was reading something I had written. At the time, I didn't give it much thought, since I was just an aspiring writer (still am). Perhaps this is that writing.

In the late 1980s, my friend Dixie went home to the arms of Jesus after an accident in her home. I miss her compassion and wisdom.

ACKNOWLEDGMENTS

Many thanks to my platoon of friends who blue-penciled, critiqued, edited, sanity-checked, and encouraged the work on this project: LeAnne Gamm, Debbie Olinger, Nikole Pennington, and Travis Scott. God brought you into my life "for such a time as this" (Esther 4:14).

I would be remiss if I didn't also give my thanks to Katie Smith, Anna Raats, and Emily Caseres, editors, all of whom have shared their knowledge and expertise with me from their years of experience editing for Ambassador International.

INTRODUCTION

During my years as a resident of Planet Earth, I've watched society decay. The decay was barely noticeable during my pre-teen years but began to accelerate during my teen years of the 1960s. In the mid '60s I joined the U.S. Navy, and the conflict in Vietnam was snuffing out the lives of combatants on both sides. The "sexual revolution" had begun among this planet's youth and was spreading even among older persons. The murder of innocent babies also became legal, mostly for convenience.

The decline of morality has been very much like being on a roller coaster approaching the pinnacle of the first drop. The coaster cars move slowly up the ramp, slowly, slowly, slowly, until the top is reached and then . . . freefall toward the bottom. Planet Earth is now in freefall mode. The Creator has lovingly given us rules to follow. We are ignoring them. If people don't wake up, the chaos of the Book of Revelation will quickly engulf us all as the final stop of our roller coaster ride.

No matter how much money or power one amasses, none of us will get out of this alive. But there is hope in living for Jesus Christ. Adonai hates sin, but He loves the sinner more. As the characters in the pages to follow come to realize, sin leads to death; but God's love, mercy and grace lead to abundant—and eternal—life. All we have to do is ask and trust what Jesus did for all mankind at Calvary.

CHAPTER 1

NEW BEGINNING

Calvin grew up in East St. Louis, a tough place to start life. He never knew his father; and his mother gave up responsibility for him to her mom when he was young, so he was raised by his grandmother. Allowing Cal to be raised by someone else was one of the few responsible things his mom ever did and likely saved Cal from a life of misery. "Nana," as he called his grandmother, was a tenderhearted, loving woman who lived what Jesus taught and led Cal in that direction as well.

Cal had his share of adolescent rebellion, but his nana managed to keep it under control; and she and Cal were able to avoid any major problems with the authorities. He was an above-average student in school; but again, it was Nana's encouragement and the attention of a high school football coach who helped him most. He was fairly good at football, just not great.

Nana took him to a non-denominational Pentecostal church every Sunday. Missing church was not allowed. Late in his junior year in high school, he met a young lady named Darlene at church. Cal was smitten instantly. When he discovered Darlene, he discovered what love felt like. And Cal really liked what it felt like to be in love. Darlene was seriously in love with Jesus, and that encouraged Cal to get serious about Him, too. Darlene was only too happy to share with Cal what she knew. They became a "thing," and life was good for Cal. Darlene was planning to go to college, but Cal didn't have enough money. He wanted to marry Darlene, but he wanted to be able to provide a good life for her before he did.

One day, late in his senior year of high school, Cal went to his Nana and said, "I think I'm going to join the army, Nana. I can get some job training and make some money at the same time. They also have what they call the G.I. Bill, which will help me pay for college when I get out. What do you think?"

"It's a good plan, Cal, and I'm proud of you for thinking about your future, but not until you graduate from high school. Who knows, that Elvis Presley boy is in the army. I think he's stationed in Germany. Maybe you'll meet him."

Her approval meant his plan was a go.

Nana and Cal were already at the bus station when Darlene arrived to see Cal off to basic training. She noticed Cal's eyes light up when he caught sight of her approaching. She smiled a wan smile back. She hoped he hadn't noticed.

Cal was headed to Fort Leonard Wood in South-Central Missouri, only about 150 miles from St. Louis.

"You look excited to be starting a new chapter in your life, Cal," Darlene said as lightheartedly as she could manage.

"I am excited, Darlene." Cal beamed. "This is just another step toward our future. Army, then college, then seminary, then we can think about our life together."

Darlene winced. *There*, she thought. *He did what I wanted to avoid today.* "One step at a time, Cal," she said. "We can't get in an all-fired hurry about the future. We have to see what the future brings. You might want to make the army a career, and I'm not sure I want to be an army wife and camp-follower."

Cal looked hurt. He'd talked about this before, and she never disagreed. In fact, she'd never said anything about it at all.

Nana spoke up. "Calvin, I've told you before not to make assumptions for other people. You do what the Lord directs, and He'll take care of all the details. Just trust in Him. You know what He said in Proverbs 3: 'lean not unto thine own understanding.' Now, let this girl be and just be glad she's here to see you off."

Darlene was grateful for Nana's running interference. She thought no one would know what was on her mind; but when she looked at Nana, she thought, *Nana knows.*

Cal looked at his Nana and said, "Yes, ma'am." Then, he said to Darlene, "Thanks for coming to see me off, Darlene. I appreciate all you've done for me."

As Darlene said, "You're welcome," the announcement for his bus to load was heard. Cal gave his nana a hug. He turned and gave Darlene a hug. Then he picked up his bag and boarded the bus to this new chapter in his life in the army.

Nana and Darlene waved to him as his bus pulled away.

———————————.✦.———

Eric had only been in Stuttgart, Germany, for a day when he met a young African-American man named Cal, one of his roommates. It was clear to Eric that Cal was different than the other soldiers in his unit, and not just that he was black. He was always smiling and he never seemed to complain, even when he got the less desirable details. His quiet time would find him sitting alone reading his Bible. The Bible thing got him loads of ribbing from the other soldiers. Cal would just smile at them and say, "I'm praying for you." When they found they couldn't ruffle his feathers, they left him alone. The only way Eric could describe him was that Cal had an inner peace and nothing seemed to bother him.

Although Eric would never admit it to anyone else, he wanted the peace Cal seemed to have. Eric hated being away from his wife and little boy. He worried that his wife, Julie, would find someone else while he was gone. He was crazy about Julie. He worried that his "little E," as he called his namesake son, would not remember him when he got back in eighteen months. Worry, worry, worry. Worrying about the many "what ifs" occupied too many of Eric's waking hours!

When the other soldiers weren't around, Eric started talking to Cal. It was just small talk, at first, warming him up to get to what he really wanted to know: why was Cal different? Eric just didn't want any of the other soldiers to know what he was seeking. He still wanted to fit in with the others. Maybe something would rub off without much effort on Eric's part.

Eric and his family had gone to church when he was growing up, and he considered himself a Christian; but there was very little effort involved or required by his church. Show up to church on Sunday and live your life doing as you pleased during the week, even if it shattered the Ten Commandments—just show up for church on Sunday. Calling yourself a "Christian" was seen by many in his family's church as a license to be disobedient to God's laws. They would quote what Jesus told Paul in 2 Corinthians 12:9: "My grace is sufficient for thee." But Eric couldn't identify with Cal's peace. What did Cal have that was missing from Eric's beliefs?

Maybe Cal knew a shortcut. Maybe Cal would share that shortcut with Eric. He could certainly use some of the peace Cal had.

Julie was a pretty young woman with light brown eyes and long strawberry-blonde hair, which she wore in a ponytail at home but let hang loose when she went out in public. And she was trim, despite having borne a son eighteen months earlier. Julie would turn twenty-one next week. Her husband, Eric, was away serving in the U.S. Army in Germany. She resented his being gone, especially over her special twenty-first birthday.

She felt trapped at home with a toddler and yearned for another adult with whom to talk. "I'm fluent in toddler speak," she often said, but she no longer felt qualified to have a decent conversation with another adult. She longed for a break from her boring life, felt desperate, and wanted a flash of excitement—even for a few hours. Surely, she thought, her mom would watch little Eric if she went out "with friends" to celebrate her birthday, so she planned her own little birthday celebration even though she didn't really have any "friends" with whom she could be festive.

Her birthday arrived, and she dropped Eric at her mother's. Mom said it would be better if the baby spent the night with her, rather than waking him when she returned. Julie agreed but not without a brief (and insincere) hesitation.

She drove to a popular bar she had heard about. It was crowded and noisy. She saw a table with three women and an empty seat. "May I join you?" she asked.

The other women looked at one another and agreed. Julie sat down and a waitress came by to take orders. Julie remained quiet as she felt out of place with nothing to contribute to the conversation. These were young women with jobs that ended around five p.m. while hers was a twenty-four/seven ordeal Julie felt the others probably wouldn't understand, so she mostly just listened to the others who never bothered to ask Julie about herself.

Occasionally, a man would come by the table to visit, and the other women would brush him off. One by one, the other women made their exits; and within a couple of hours, Julie was left alone at the table with half of the glass of wine she had bought for herself when she first arrived.

An attractive man in his mid-to-late twenties, wearing what Julie thought must be an expensive suit and tie, offered to buy her a drink and asked to join her. She agreed. He introduced himself as Matt. She started to feel the excitement she had long missed—and felt she needed—as they talked and drank. She was not used to alcohol and soon felt its effects.

Julie told Matt that she needed to leave because she was feeling woozy. He asked if she was okay to drive and offered to follow her home to make sure she got there safely. She agreed. She arrived home, and Matt walked her to the door of her apartment.

"May I come in?" he asked.

Julie didn't want the excitement to end, so she agreed. *No one will ever know,* she thought to herself.

As Julie was waking, she felt a throbbing pain behind her eyes. Her mouth felt parched and dry. As she became more alert, she remembered. She jerked her head to see if she was alone in her bed. The head jerk made the pain behind her eyes explode. But the good news was that she was alone.

She stumbled to her bathroom to get something wet for the scorching desert in her mouth. The cold water felt good, but gulping it down felt even better. *Alcohol dehydrates,* she thought. *Too much wine.*

She went to her living room. No Matt—and she was glad. She looked in the kitchen—again, no Matt. She looked for a note. No note. He had just walked away in the middle of the night with no thought of how it might feel to her, and she suddenly felt more alone than she could ever remember feeling. She wondered how she could be so elated he was gone but feel so abandoned and unhappy that he'd left so secretly.

She fell into her couch and began to sob. She had given herself to him, and he had thrown her away like a piece of garbage. She cried even harder at the thought of being cast aside so casually.

"Oh," she groaned, "what have I done?" How would this affect her husband and her son? She realized that she had been wrong about no one ever knowing. She knew. And knowing was painful—more painful than she had imagined it could be.

With whom could she talk? Her mom? She and her mom weren't really that close. Certainly not her husband. He would never understand *this* betrayal. Most of her "close" friends from high school were away at college and had moved on from friendship with her. The only friend she had ever shared the closeness she needed now was Cathy. Julie remembered how she and Cathy had talked endlessly about everything. She recalled too, however, that she and Cathy hadn't parted on the best of terms. Julie frowned at herself as she recalled being nasty with her old friend the last time they had seen one another.

How would Cathy react to what Julie had to talk about? Julie and Cathy had drifted apart after Cathy "got religion." Cathy had invited her to church, but Julie just didn't think church was cool. Cathy seemed happy all the time, and Julie was glad for her; but church just didn't fit into Julie's plans.

Julie thought about what she had done last night. That certainly didn't fit into her plans either. Julie decided she needed a new plan, but she also needed a friend like Cathy to put that new plan together—just like they did in the old days. Julie wondered if Cathy would even talk to her. She also wondered if she'd ever feel clean again.

Matt waited until Julie's breathing told him that she was really asleep. He eased out of her bed, picked up his clothes, went into the living room, dressed, and let himself out. This was *not* his first round-up. Matt had first seen this behavior from the men his mother had brought home when he was a kid—men seen once, then never again. This was the way it was supposed to be, wasn't it? One and done.

His mother and father had weathered a stormy marriage with constant fighting and turmoil. After they divorced, his mother had often told Matt, "Thankfully, you're the only kid out of that mess." He had never felt loved by his mom. He was pretty much on his own, since she was rarely there for him. She was usually at some bar partying until the wee hours, and then she'd drag home yet another man.

Matt was abandoned physically and emotionally by his mother and his worldview had hatched from his childhood experiences.

It was through Matt's own grit and determination that he had put himself through college, then law school. He had to depend on himself because there was no one else to whom he could turn. Based on his parents' example of parenting and adulthood, Matt was justifiably terrified of a marriage of his own which might be as topsy-turvy as his parents' marriage had been. He gave no thought about what he might be doing to the emotions of others. He gave no thought about tomorrow. All he had was now. Plans? What's the point? Love 'em and leave 'em. One-night wives.

CHAPTER 2
BOOMERANG

Matt had been visiting his favorite bar and hunting ground nearly every night for three weeks with no luck. Not even a nibble. He tried to remember the last time he had scored—it was that cute, little Julie chick with the long hair. She was a lot better-looking than most of the girls he was able to snag and drag.

Maybe he should go to a different bar, file a change of venue. He smiled at his own lawyer joke. Or, he thought to himself, maybe he should violate his own rules and revisit Julie. She was easy.

Although Julie hadn't talked about it, Matt knew she had a kid because of the toys laying around her apartment. He didn't mind a kid as long as the kid kept out of his way. He didn't know if she was married or not, and he didn't particularly care.

He downed the last of his drink and headed for his car. That's what he'd do: visit Julie. He knew where she lived, and it wasn't that far away. And she was good-looking.

Driving to her apartment, Matt anticipated a replay of the pleasure he'd had with her but gave no thought to the way he had ducked out after their last encounter. Surely, easy girls expected that kind of behavior from men. His mom showed him that side of things. He walked to her door and knocked.

After about a minute, he heard her voice from the other side. "Who is it?" She didn't open the door.

"Matt," was all he said.

"Get lost, creep!" she shouted.

"Wait, can't I come in and talk?"

"No! Get lost. And never come back here!"

"Come on, Julie. Let's just talk."

"No! I told you to get lost, and I meant it."

Matt stood there quietly for a minute and then turned and went back to his car. A change of venue would definitely be the thing to do now.

For several days, Cathy wrestled with thoughts about her high school friend, Julie. They were almost inseparable once. Cathy started to call Julie's mom several times to get her old friend's number but stopped short, thinking of their last visit several years back.

Cathy questioned her sudden, seemingly urgent, thoughts and concerns about her old friend. She finally gave in, knowing God sometimes puts other people on our hearts. *I don't have anything to lose,* Cathy thought as she picked up her phone to call Julie's mom. It couldn't be any worse than the last time they talked.

Cathy was pleasantly surprised at how chatty Julie's mom became when Cathy identified herself. Cathy's previous experience with Julie's mom hadn't been particularly comfortable, and Cathy wondered if her treatment had anything to do with the fact that she was the child of a mixed-race marriage. Julie's mom told her about Julie's little boy and her husband serving in the U.S. Army in Germany and other tidbits about her. Cathy listened patiently and finally got Julie's telephone number.

Jules was the name Cathy had called her friend when they were running around together. It was one of those nicknames one friend fondly calls another—a special name for a special friend in her life—and Jules had been the object of Cathy's prayers ever since the day of their fractured friendship. The phone still warm from talking with Julie's mom, Cathy phoned her friend. Julie answered.

"Hey, Jules, it's Cathy. How are you?"

There was an uneasy silence for several seconds, and Cathy wondered if she had made a mistake. Had she misunderstood the urgency she'd felt about her friend? Then she heard Julie's soft sobbing.

"Jules, are you okay?"

Through Julie's sobbing, Cathy was barely able to understand what Julie was trying to tell her. "Jules, it sounds like you could really use a friendly ear right now. Do you want me to come over, so we can talk?"

"Oh! Please do. I've needed to talk to you for several weeks." Julie gave Cathy her address.

Cathy pulled her car up to Jule's apartment building and breathed a quick prayer. "Lord Jesus, please be in this reunion, according to your will, to your eternal glory. Amen." While she was excited to see her old friend, she was also apprehensive. Julie hadn't been able to communicate well on the phone; and since Cathy knew her old friend always had something intelligent to say, she felt uneasy.

Julie answered her door, eyes red and swollen from crying. Cathy had never seen her friend look so bad. Cathy spread her arms wide for a hug, into which Julie gratefully and completely snuggled as she began crying and sobbing again. Her head nestled onto Cathy's neck, Julie began to mumble things amid sobs which Cathy couldn't decipher.

The two young women stood hugging in Julie's doorway for a few minutes until Julie broke away and invited Cathy inside. Julie's apartment was a bit messy. A little boy was playing with his trucks on the floor.

"This is Eric," Julie managed to say, pointing to the boy. "He's named after his dad."

"How do you do, Eric?" Cathy said to the boy. Cathy didn't have much experience with children, so treating him like she would another adult felt like the proper thing to do.

The boy looked at Cathy and said, "Trucks," pointing to his toys.

"They sure are," Cathy said. "And they look like nice ones." The boy beamed and went back to his imaginary truck world.

"Can I make you some coffee, Cath?" And there it was—the special nickname Julie had given her so long ago. Cathy nearly sobbed herself at hearing it.

"I'd love some," she answered.

Julie busied herself in the kitchen making the brew while Cathy sat on the couch and watched Eric *vroom* his trucks around the floor. Then Julie came back and sat sideways on the couch. She sighed heavily and started to tear up again. "I've totally messed up my life," she blurted.

Cathy listened. She had no idea where this was going, but the best thing she could do was just listen.

"I haven't had anyone to talk with like we used to. Oh, Cath, I've missed you so much. I've needed you, but I messed that up, too." And she began crying again.

Cathy moved over and put her arms around her friend. Julie cried and sobbed for a few more minutes. Cathy began to cry as well, from sheer happiness at being with her friend again and sadness, too, from Julie's apparent despair.

Julie pulled back and said, "For the past two months, I've done nothing but cry. I'm so alone with Eric in Germany, and, well, you know how my mom is. I can't really talk to her. The only person I have to talk to is little Eric, and his communication skills are . . . well . . . if you can't talk about his trucks or what's for lunch, don't bother."

Cathy nodded but didn't truly understand.

"And now, I'm really in a mess. I don't know how to tell you . . . or anyone . . ." Julie's voice trailed off. "I'm facing the biggest problem I've ever had to face. And I don't know what to do because I don't know how it's going to turn out. I've never been in a fix like this before!"

Both women were quiet for a minute, Cathy trying to figure out what to say and Julie trying to figure out whether she should tell her friend the reason for her pain and anguish, whether or not to tell her everything.

Then Cathy got an idea. "Julie, I don't know all the details of your troubles—and maybe it's none of my business—but if you don't feel comfortable telling me but need someone to talk to, maybe try praying."

Julie began to protest, but Cathy cut her short. "Now before you bull-up and have a fit, just consider something. Have you ever gone through an automatic car wash where you go through a tunnel affair? When you go in, there are signs that tell you to put the car in neutral, keep your foot off the brake, and keep your hands off the steering wheel. Those rules are put there for our safety. As your car goes through the tunnel and soap and chemicals are dropped on the outside of the car, you can't see where you and the car are headed. You just have to trust that the rules and the bigger picture of a properly operating machine will keep you on the right path and lead to safety at the other end."

"I don't see how that applies to me, Cath. What does a car wash have to do with it?"

"That's how prayer works. We don't know all the answers, but God does. Trust Him, Jules." Cathy hoped she hadn't confused the issue without really knowing any of the details. "Never mind that right now. I'll explain later. Just tell me what you feel comfortable telling me, and we'll try to figure it out together. Okay?"

It was going to be a boring evening around the barracks with Cal getting stuck answering the "duty phone"—charge of quarters duty in another barracks until midnight. Eric opened the Bible Cal had given him, but reading it by himself just wouldn't be the same without Cal there to guide him and to explain things Eric didn't understand or had questions about.

Just then, Eric's buddy Skip stuck his head through Eric's door and said, "Hey, Eric, wanna' go to the EM club with us and spend some of your payday cash?"

Eric didn't have much "payday cash" to spare, since he sent most of his money home to Julie. Eric thought about it for a few seconds. *I could probably use the break*, he thought. "Sure, let me put some clothes on," he said.

A few minutes later, Eric flew out his door to catch up with the other soldiers headed to the Enlisted Men's club. "There's going to be a band tonight," Skip announced. That usually brings out the local girls. Could be a good night, boys. A plenteous stable of local talent to choose from." He smirked.

"Aren't you married, Skip?" Eric subtly reminded him.

"Yup, sure am." Skip replied with a wink. "That doesn't stop me from lookin', though."

When they arrived, the band was already playing; and the club was packed with dancers, wannabe dancers, and those avoiding the dance floor altogether and just sitting at the tables drinking their German beer. Eric and his buddies looked for an empty table but didn't spot any right away. As the others looked for a place to plant themselves, Skip disappeared for a few minutes but returned to tell his friends to follow him.

Skip wound his way through the noisy throng to a table with four girls sitting by themselves. Eric wasn't interested in the girls, but a place to sit was still better than standing around all night. The soldiers snagged an empty chair each and sat at the table with the girls.

Skip disappeared again and returned carrying two pitchers of beer in one hand and four glass beer mugs in the other. "These German boys know how to make beer." He put the pitchers and mugs on the table and began pouring mugs of beer and dealing them out to his friends. "First round is on me," he said, "but we all need to kick in from here on out."

Eric's friends paired off with the girls at the table, which suited Eric just fine. He wanted to stay true to his wife. He'd just drink a few beers and head back to the barracks.

Before long, another girl arrived who seemed to know the others. She spoke loudly to the other girls in German. Eric didn't speak much German, but she seemed unhappy that there was no place for her to sit. Eric gallantly offered her his chair. He could always try to find another one. When he stood, she wrapped her arms around him and gave him a long kiss on his lips. It was as though someone had hit him on the head with a club; he was stunned by her boldness.

"You sit down, Joe," she said. "I just sit on your lap."

"No, my name's Eric." He wasn't aware that local girls called American G.I.s "Joe" until they found the necessity to actually learn their name. "Let me find another chair," he said.

She assumed a fake frown. "You not want Christina to sit on your lap?"

"No, it's not that . . . "

"Then sit and we get to know us." And she sat on his lap and snuggled up to him with an arm around his neck. As much as Eric wanted to object, he liked her sweet aroma and the way she felt sitting on his lap. The more beer he drank, the more he decided to just go with it. She kissed him full on his mouth multiple times. The more she kissed him, the more he liked her—and her kisses.

They drank beer, danced, and laughed until the band quit at eleven p.m. Many beers later, when the band stopped playing, Skip said, "Hey, guys, let's go get a tattoo."

Eric had never thought much about getting a tattoo; but in his impaired condition, he agreed to go with them. All five girls went, too.

The tattoo episode became a fog. He didn't remember choosing a design. He vaguely felt the needle puncturing his skin, but it didn't seem to hurt nearly as much he'd heard others say it did. They left the tattoo parlor, and Christina took his hand and held him back from the others.

"You come with Christina," she breathed in his ear. "No one will ever know."

As he woke up, Eric's head felt as big and hot as the state of Texas in July. He wanted to groan but was afraid it would make his head hurt worse than it already did. His upper right arm felt like it was on fire. He reached over with his left hand and discovered a series of hot, painful bumps there. He pulled his hand back because it hurt to touch the spot. He hadn't opened his eyes yet, but he wondered where he was. Warily, he opened one eye.

Whew. It was his room at the barracks. But how did he get here? He didn't remember. Why did he feel so bad? Then he remembered and groaned. "Oh, no. What have I done?"

He saw Cal sitting at his desk, smiling. Eric thought he must have heard his groan and looked up from his Bible reading to greet his friend.

"How are you feeling this morning, buddy?" Cal asked. "You were a mess last night."

"I'm not in much better shape this morning, Cal."

Cal chuckled. "That's the way it is with misbehaving. My nana says misbehaving takes you places you ought not to be and wish you'd never been when you get there. She says we don't need to worry about the big sins gettin' us if we stand against the little sins. You do the little ones enough you get numb to 'em; and they just keep gettin' bigger and bigger until they got you sure enough."

"What day is today?" Eric wanted to know.

"Saturday."

That was a relief. At least, he hadn't missed any duty. That would have been even worse trouble than his headache and sore arm. He looked at his arm. It was fire red around a black Maltese Cross.

"Oh, no!" Eric moaned. "A tattoo. Now, I remember."

"Yup," Cal chuckled. "Those things happen when you let your guard down like you did last night."

"Aren't you mad at me, Cal?"

"Gettin' mad at you wouldn't do no good, for you or me. I'm not your judge; I'm your friend, and friends stand by each other. That's why I made sure you got home last night without the MPs doin' a tap dance on you."

"Well, that explains how I got here. But where did you find me?"

"Well, I was coming back from CQ and saw you staggering around with that German girl Christina, who was hollerin' at you about you owing her twenty dollars."

"Twenty dollars? For what?"

Cal chuckled again. "You must be the only guy on post that don't know a date with Christina comes with a twenty-dollar price tag. I'll let you do the math."

"I don't remember . . . but I didn't have twenty dollars, Cal."

"Well, I did, so I paid her and got you back here."

"Thanks, buddy. I owe you."

"I figure the way you feel will keep you on the path you need to stay on." Cal smiled and chuckled again.

CHAPTER 3
SPILLING THE BEANS

As the pent-up emotions behind the dam Julie had built for herself burst, pouring out the guilt, pain, remorse, anger, and sorrow of her twenty-first birthday celebration, it was like Cathy was watching a swollen mountain stream midway through the spring melt. Cathy did her best to not show anything but sincere concern for her friend, but it was hard for her to not start crying herself.

"And the worst of it is now I'm pregnant. My husband has been in Germany for three months and won't be home for another fifteen months." Julie began crying again. "The baby would be born way before Eric got back," she said through her tears. Cathy was quiet, waiting for more.

"I can only see one way out of this," Julie continued. "Get rid of the baby." There was a silence between them for several minutes until Julie broke it. "Aren't you going to say anything, Cath? Aren't you going to preach to me? Tell me abortion is murder?" Julie was crying again. "Aren't you going to tell me I'm going to Hell?"

"Jesus tells me to love my neighbor. If I behaved the way you expect me to, I would be disobedient to my Lord. We all make mistakes, Jules. I've certainly made my share."

"Yeah," Julie replied, "but these are doozies. But wait, there's more."

Cathy wanted to groan but kept it in. What else could there be?

"I tracked the creep down and told him I was going to have his baby. He said, 'I'm a lawyer. Good luck pinning that on me.'" Julie began crying again. "And the worst part of that confrontation is he and his buddies laughed at me. Those dirtbags just added more shame to what I was already feeling. What else can I do?"

"Remember the analogy I gave you about the car wash?" Cathy asked.

Julie nodded.

"Being a Christian is a lot like that. If we obey the rules, keep our foot off the brake and our hands off the steering wheel, and trust in *His* outcome, we'll arrive safely at the end of the tunnel. God wants the best for us because He loves us. Jesus told a story about God's eye being on the sparrow. He loves us far more than sparrows; if His eye is on the sparrow, how much more is His attention drawn to you and me?"

"I wish I could be sure of that," Julie said. "But what I need from you right now is not Bible stories. Help me to hatch a plan like we did when we were young." A weak smile crossed Julie's face. "We sure had fun, didn't we?"

"We did," Cathy agreed, "but let me fill you in on a plan already in the works. I'm going out to my car for a minute. I'll be right back."

———————.✦⁺.———

Eric was going to have to "beat feet" to make it back to his job at the motor pool on time after lunch break. He needed to get two batteries out of his foot locker in the barracks before returning to work. As he entered the barracks, he heard someone sobbing. He looked in his room, but no one was there. He got in his locker, grabbed the batteries, and tried to make a hasty retreat. But the crying and sobbing got louder.

"I don't have time for this," Eric exclaimed as he began searching for the source of the woeful wail. He began walking slowly down the corridor until he came to a utility closet. The noise was coming from inside. Eric opened the door.

"Cal!" Eric exclaimed. Tears were streaming down Cal's face, and he couldn't stop sobbing. Cal was on his knees in front of a deep sink as though he'd been praying. "What's wrong, buddy?"

Cal managed to mumble "Darlene" through his sobs, and he handed Eric a letter he had crumpled in his hand. Eric read the letter Cal had received from his girl. The classic "Dear John." Darlene had met a man in college. Of course, she never intended to hurt Cal, but she and her college friend planned to be married in the early summer. And she was sorry. Eric felt pain for his friend.

"Oh, man! That's cold," was all Eric could say. He didn't know what else to say. His friend was in pain. Eric had never seen Cal in pain and didn't know how to deal with it. He put his hand on Cal's shoulder. "Is there anything I can do?" Eric grimaced at his lame question. What in the world could he possibly do to ease his friend's pain?

Cal shook his head. Eric needed to get back to the motor pool, but he also needed to be with Cal. What a quandary! "I need to get back to work, but we need to deal with this. How do we do it, buddy?"

Cal had nearly stopped sobbing and said, "You go back to work. We can talk about this later."

Cathy returned from her car carrying two Bibles. "I bought this Bible for you a long time ago," she said, holding up a white Bible for

Julie to see. "And I've kept it, hoping this day would come: the day I give it to you. I even had your name engraved on it."

Julie groaned. "Come on, Cath, not the Bible stuff again."

"Jules," Cathy took a serious tone, "you said you wanted a plan." Cathy looked Julie straight in the eye. "And you also asked for my help. I'm showing you the way to the *perfect* plan for life. If you continue to go your own way, I can't help you. No one can help you. Only Jesus can."

Julie was quiet for several minutes but so was Cathy, waiting for her to say something—anything. Julie finally broke the silence. "Okay, Cath. I'll listen, but I don't think it's for me."

"Lots of people say that same thing. The reality is that it's for everyone, not just a few."

"So, where do we start, Cath? Sodom and Gomorrah?"

"Oh, you know about that, do you? See, you already know more than I thought you did. No, we're going to start in Jeremiah."

"Where's that?" Julie wanted to know."

"It's not a physical location; it's a book in the Bible written by an Old Testament prophet named Jeremiah about six hundred years before Jesus Christ was born."

"Cath, that's more than twenty-five hundred years ago. How can that be even remotely relevant today?"

"Good question. It's relevant today because God's promises are timeless. Much of Jeremiah's prophecy was about the birth and life of Jesus Christ. Prophecies which were fulfilled. Another prophecy of his predicted the fall of Jerusalem, which was also came about."

"Okay, so he got lucky . . . a lot."

"Now, listen to this. From Jeremiah 29:11-13: 'For I know the thoughts that I think toward you, saith the LORD, thoughts of peace and not of evil, to give you an expected end. Then shall ye call upon me, and ye shall go and pray unto me, and I will hearken unto you. And ye shall seek me, and find me, when ye shall search for me with all your heart.' This is one of my favorite promises God has given us."

Julie was quiet again. She searched Cathy's smiling face for some hint, some clue, that she didn't truly believe what she was sharing. She found none.

"The Bible is filled with God's promises to us," Cathy continued. "You wanted a plan. God's plan for you from this point on is the perfect plan."

"Okay, so why didn't He keep all this from happening to me?" Julie asked.

"The best I can figure is He had to get your attention first. Would you have listened if these things hadn't happened to you?"

Julie gave Cathy's last statement a long thought. "Probably not," was all she could say.

The ringing of Cathy's phone woke her from a sound sleep. She looked at her alarm clock on the nightstand next to the bed: 2:17 a.m. *What in the world?* Her sleepy voice croaked, "Hello?"

"Cathy, I'm sorry to bother you at this late hour. This is Barb. Julie's mom. She's in the hospital and not doing well."

The news snapped Cathy to attention. "Why? What's going on?"

"Julie told me last weeks about her troubles. I was furious at her for doing this to me. So, I told her to get an abortion. The sooner, the better. I didn't want my friends to find out. She lost a lot of blood after her procedure today, and we had to take her to the emergency room."

Cathy was stunned. She hadn't talked with Jules for several days, but their conversations had led Cathy to believe that Jules had given up on the idea of getting an abortion. Now this! She felt anger swelling inside her, not only at Julie for what she had done to that innocent baby but also at Barb for hanging an emotional anchor on her daughter by claiming Julie's problems were only done to harm her mom. How self-centered! Cathy had trouble holding back, but she managed.

"Where is she? Who has little Eric? Can I see her?" Cathy's questions spilled out.

"She's at Cheyenne Regional Medical Center, and you can see her tomorrow afternoon. I have Eric. He wants his mommy—and his trucks, which I made him leave at home. He's such a boy. He never picks up after himself."

By now, Cathy's tongue was nearly in shreds from her holding it. Cathy ended the call and began to cry. For Julie. For the innocent baby. For Julie's mom. And for herself. Julie didn't know it, but she had killed what Cathy could never have—a baby.

Then, Cathy bowed her head. "Lord Jesus, please forgive me for being judgmental. And thank You for Your grace and forgiveness."

CHAPTER 4
NO CAN DO!

Eric hurried back to the motor pool knowing he was going to be late. He tried to slip in unnoticed, but his hawk-eyed first shirt, Sergeant Tiller, didn't miss much.

"Corporal. You're late. Is your job interfering with your social life, lad?" Sergeant Tiller wanted to know.

"Sorry, Sarge," Eric apologized. "My buddy Cal is having a bad day, and I just needed to help him out a little bit."

"So, your Bible-thumping Mr. Smiley Cal's got problems, huh? What's wrong? Did they cancel church on Sunday?"

"Come on, Sarge. Give the guy a break. His girl sent him a 'Dear John' letter. He's pretty bummed out about it. I was going to see if I could finish up the brake job I'm doing and head on back to give him some moral support."

The sergeant studied Eric for a few seconds, then grumbled, "I don't really see how we can spare you here. We've got too much work to get done, and Jones is going on leave tomorrow. No can do."

Eric hustled back to his work station but had trouble keeping his head in the vehicle maintenance game. He had to figure some way to help his friend, short of going AWOL. He thought about how he would feel if Julie sent him that kind of letter. He shuddered at the thought of losing her and not seeing his little "E" very often—or even never! There had to be some way for him to help his buddy.

He finished the brake job and drove the Jeep to the lot in the rear of the vehicle maintenance building. *Maybe*, Eric thought, *Sarge will let me go now.*

He hurried back to the sergeant's desk with only two hours left until his four P.M. quitting time; but before he could ask to leave, Sarge flashed a mean-looking smile and told him that General Short's car needed a complete tune-up. Eric's first inclination was to grumble and whine, but he didn't. He remembered what Cal always said: "Don't do what people expect from you. Be nice. Just go with the flow. The more we complain, the more life gives us to complain about."

Eric smiled and said, "Sure, Sarge," and took the keys Sarge had in his hand. Eric was inwardly pleased that Sarge looked puzzled.

Eric finished the general's car about 1630 and parked the car next to the Jeep he'd finished earlier. He headed to the first sergeant's desk, but Sarge was gone. He put General Short's keys on the desk, locked up, and headed back to the barracks to look for Cal.

Cal was not there, and no one he asked had seen him since before lunch. Eric's first thought was that Cal had gone "over the hill"—AWOL—but Eric couldn't see Cal *ever* doing that. Where was he?

Cathy struggled with thoughts about whether or not to get Jules flowers and, if she did, what kind. Carnations were colorful and inexpensive—some would say cheap. And definitely no stuffed animal. She finally decided to just go with a get-well card.

Cathy walked into Julie's hospital room and nearly gasped at her friend looking so pale and gaunt. She was relieved to find that Julie's mom was not there. Julie wouldn't look Cathy in the eye. It was as if Jules was trying to hide from her.

"How are you feeling, Jules?" she asked cheerily as she handed her friend the get-well card. She had tried to find a card that was middle-of-the-road—not too funny but not too somber, either. This porridge needed to be "just right."

"I guess my mom called you to tell on me," Julie said, tossing aside the card Cathy had brought without opening it. "So, what now? Are you going to write me off like God probably has? Like my mom has? Like Eric probably will? I thought nobody would ever know what I did, but he's going to find out about this—I'm sure of it—and then my life will be ruined, for sure."

Cathy just stood by her friend's bedside silently praying for guidance to handle what her friend was feeling. "Do you want me to pray with you, Jules? I'd be happy to."

"No. No prayer. Your God let me down. I'm done."

"All right, then. Do you want me to leave?"

"Yes, that would be best. You can't help me."

"You're right," Cathy replied trying to hold her anger, and tears, in check. "I can't help you because you need to want to help yourself first. I'll leave; but before I do, I want you to know that yesterday, you threw away something I want but can never have of my own—a baby. My body is incapable of having one because I had cervical cancer last year. Surgery to deal with cancer fixed it so I can never have kids. So, while you lie in that hospital bed feeling sorry for yourself and blaming God and everyone but yourself for your situation, you need to start accepting responsibility for the things *you* do. As long as you are playing the blame game, nobody can help you. I'm sorry for you, Julie. Goodbye."

Cathy left, went to her car, and began crying for her friend. And then she prayed for her.

After nearly an hour on his knees in the broom closet, Cal pulled himself together enough to go see the base chaplain. The chaplain just happened to be a Jewish rabbi. Cal had spoken with the rabbi on several occasions and found him to be a very kind and compassionate man, and Cal liked him.

Cal entered the base chapel and asked the young female working there if the chaplain was in. She was a civilian, so Cal assumed she must be the dependent of another soldier.

"He won't be back for about twenty minutes," she told him in a decidedly indifferent tone.

"May I wait? It's pretty important."

She studied him for a second and said, "Suit yourself. Have a chair."

After Cal had waited for nearly thirty minutes, the chaplain returned.

"This man would like to see you, sir," the receptionist said dully, pointing to Cal.

Rabbi Cohen turned and, recognizing Cal from previous conversations, said, "Well, greetings, my young Ethiopian friend."

Cal loved the rabbi's easy and sometimes confusing way of talking. "Hello, Rabbi. Can I have a few minutes of your time?" Cal hoped his eyes weren't too bloodshot.

"Certainly, just give me a few minutes to make a quick phone call, and my ears are all yours." He disappeared into his office, closing his door.

About ten minutes later, the rabbi reappeared at his office door and said, "Come in, young man. Let's visit. I've wanted to talk with you, anyway."

Cal accepted the invitation and the chair the rabbi offered as he closed his office door. The rabbi returned to his desk chair and said, "How may I assist you today? Your red eyes tell me you have a problem."

Cal stared to choke-up again as he handed him the letter from Darlene. As the rabbi read Darlene's letter, a pained look crossed his face. He looked up at Cal and, with sadness in his voice, said, "That's a thorny bush, isn't it?"

Cal couldn't choke the word out, so he just nodded.

"How long have you known your young lady?" Still unable to talk, Cal held up two fingers. "Two months?" Cal shook his head, no. "Two years?" This time, he nodded.

"Hmm. This constitutes 'woman's inhumanity to man,'" Rabbi Cohen said, intentionally misquoting the old indictment on inhumanity. "How long have you been in the army?"

Cal was finally able to croak, "Just over a year."

"What do you want me to do?" the rabbi asked. "Do you want to go home on leave to straighten things out? Do you want a pass to get your head together? Just tell me, and I'll see if I can arrange it."

"I just need some time alone," Cal managed to say. "None of the guys in the barracks, except Eric, understand me. If I rent a hotel room for a day or two to read my Bible and pray, the Lord will help me figure this thing out. I just need to be left alone to do it."

The rabbi nodded and said, "I'll do my best to arrange that. In the meantime, would you like a word of prayer?"

Cal gave him a quizzical look. Rabbi Cohen smiled and said, "Yes, I'm a rabbi, but I'm also what is known as a 'completed Jew.' I accept Jesus Christ as the long-awaited Messiah. As a rabbi, I've extensively studied what you call the Old Testament and what we Jews call the 'Law and the Prophets.' And I've determined for myself that the prophecies in the Old Testament point directly to Jesus Christ as Messiah. That makes me unacceptable to the Jews to serve as a rabbi, but I can serve as a chaplain in the military. Here in the army, I can pray the Shema, and celebrate the Passover and the other high holy days with Jewish soldiers, and pray the Lord's Prayer, and celebrate Easter and Christmas with the Christians. Now, would you like for me to pray with you?"

Cal smiled for the first time since he got Darlene's letter and, nodding, bowed his head.

"Abba Father," the chaplain began, "our awesome heavenly Daddy, El Shaddai, the Great I Am, my friend Cal and I approach Your throne today with heavy hearts and ask that You comfort him and show him the path You have chosen for him to follow. We ask You, Jehovah Shalom, to grant him Your peace in the process. In the precious Name of our Lord and risen Savior Jesus Christ, we pray. Amen."

Cal heaved a huge sigh, releasing an inner pressure he'd been experiencing. He smiled at the chaplain and said, "What a great prayer! I love the way you pray not only Scripture, but also God's names."

The chaplain smiled. "I like to pray the names of God because His names testify to His character and promises, and to the fact that we can trust His wisdom."

Cal nodded in agreement and then furrowed his brow and asked, "I'm curious, Rabbi, why do you call me your 'Ethiopian friend'? I'm from East Saint Louis."

The chaplain smiled again and said, "That's a great question, Cal, and you can just call me Chaplain. You see, in Moses' later years, after his first wife died, he married an Ethiopian woman. Moses' sister, Miriam, and his brother bad-mouthed her because she was black, but I suspect Miriam was the lead busybody here because she's the one whom God afflicted with leprosy. She was only afflicted for seven days; but I want no part of leprosy for even one day, so it helps me to remember to treat everyone the same, regardless of our differences."

"Thanks, Rabbi—er, Chaplain. Jesus taught that we should love everyone the same, too. I've read the whole Bible, but I sure missed the significance of why Miriam was struck with leprosy. Thanks."

"You're welcome," the chaplain said. "Now, let me get to work on some alone time for you. When you get back from your 'getaway,' I'll want to have another chat with you. I think you and I can help each other quite a bit, if you're interested. But that can wait until you have a clear head."

Cal nodded without knowing exactly to what he was agreeing; but he trusted the chaplain, and that was good enough.

CHAPTER 5
CHAPLAIN JACOB COHEN'S STORY

Jacob grew up in New York City in an Orthodox Jewish family. His family was fastidious about keeping the Sabbath and all High Holy Days. Jacob's favorite Jewish festival was the Passover. He loved the taste of lamb, which he always associated with the Seder feast.

When it was time for Jacob to attend Hebrew school, he was elated. He absolutely devoured everything he could lay his hands on about Jewish history, traditions and language. He never seemed to get enough, a fact which pleased his parents and his rabbi mentor. He loved the Law and pored over the Prophets and Psalms with vigor, and he could quote much of it from memory.

After high school, Jacob had attended Yeshiva University on the lower East Side of New York and earned a bachelor's degree in Jewish Studies. After graduation, he had moved to the Jewish Theological Seminary to become a rabbi. All through his formal education, he was particularly enamored with Scriptures dealing with Messianic prophecy and studied them tirelessly. But in the final year of his studies at Jewish Theological Seminary, he had begun to ask himself, what if his Hebrew fathers had missed the Messiah? What if the

Messiah really was Jesus, known as the Christ? But how could he know for sure?

He went to a Christian bookstore shopping for a Christian Holy Bible and purchased a King James Version. He read through the four Gospels several times but was most mesmerized by the Gospel according to John. The other three were interesting, especially Matthew's treatment of the lineage of Jesus; but John's Gospel gave him the greatest joy.

Jacob cross-referenced the Prophets and Psalms with the accounts of Jesus' life, crucifixion, and death and came to the conclusion that Jesus was, indeed, the long-awaited Messiah! How could any of his ancestors have missed it? The clues were everywhere in the Law, Psalms, and the Prophets; but he was particularly taken with Psalm 22, written by King David one thousand years before Jesus was born. Psalm 22 says in part in verse sixteen, "They pierced my hands and my feet," and in verse eighteen, "They part my garments among them, and cast lots upon my vesture." And Jacob was aware that those things actually happened at Calvary's cross.

He decided to investigate his findings more fully by attending Christian churches of various denominations outside "the city with a million altars to idols," which is what he called New York. He purchased several sets of new clothes to more readily fit into the gentile groups with whom he intended to visit. He drove to small towns at least seventy-five miles outside New York City to avoid groups that might be too materialistic. He drove to the location he had chosen for that week on Saturday, after his own Jewish services were complete, checked into a motel, and studied for his classes, and read his New Testament. He read Hebrews over and over. What a joy.

Jacob was more than a little surprised that with most of the churches he visited, very few, if any, of the members welcomed him; but after each Christian service was concluded, Jacob always introduced himself to the pastor and explained that he was a rabbinical student from the seminary and wanted to ask a few questions. He found some pastors were downright rude and acted like he was unwelcome scum. Others dodged his questions and told him to study his own texts for the answers he sought. Some didn't act like they knew the answers to his simple questions and gave him the brush-off. It wasn't until he attended an Assembly of God Church that he hit the mother lode. At least two dozen people introduced themselves and welcomed him.

That's refreshing he thought.

After the service, Jacob joined the queue to pay respects to the pastor. "Hi, my name is Jacob, and I'm a student in my final year at Jewish Theological Seminary in New York," he told the pastor of the small white church well outside the reaches of New York City.

The pastor gave Jacob a huge smile and said, "Welcome, my friend. I'm Pastor Phil. I hope you enjoyed today's message."

"Yes, I did. You answered a couple of questions I had in your sermon, but I have a couple more I'd like to ask."

"And I'd like to answer them," he replied. "Could you give me a few minutes to greet my congregation first?"

"Absolutely. I'll just wait until you're finished," said Jacob. He went and sat on a bench near the front door, where he watched the middle-aged, graying-at-the-temples Pastor Phil as he loved and shepherded Jesus' flock that had been entrusted to him. It was a pleasure for Jacob to see this man focus his full attention on each person who greeted him, and it made him smile to watch. Pastor Phil appeared to be the genuine article. There didn't seem to be anything phony about him.

After about ten minutes, the pastor finished his "meet and greet" and said, "I have about twenty minutes before I have to scoot. Do you want to visit here, or would you rather go to my office?"

"Talking here is fine," Jacob replied as he rose from the bench where he'd been sitting. "First, in the Gospel of John, Jesus is baptized by his cousin, John the Baptist. I'm curious, since salvation is through the shed blood, death, and resurrection of Jesus Christ, why does the Christian Church still baptize today? Baptism doesn't save anyone."

"Wow," Pastor Phil said. "That's a well-reasoned question. I like it. We still baptize today in the modern church for several reasons. One, out of obedience. The children of Israel have a long history of disobedience to Yahweh. That disobedience led to many harsh consequences for them. We have chosen to be obedient. If baptism is good enough for our Savior, it's good enough for us. And reason two is explained by Paul in Galatians 3:27-29: 'For as many of you as have been baptized into Christ have put on Christ. There is neither Jew nor Greek, there is neither bond nor free, there is neither male nor female: for ye are all one in Christ Jesus. And if ye be Christ's, then are ye Abraham's seed, and heirs according to the promise.' Thirdly is Colossians 2:12, where Paul explains that we were circumcised when we were 'buried with him in baptism' and were 'risen with him through the faith of the operation of God, who hath raised him from the dead.'"

Jacob nodded. "Good answer, Pastor. Also, I hear Christians bouncing the terms 'gospel' and 'good news' around like they're some kind of secret code words without anyone ever taking the time to define them, at least from what I've heard. What's your definition?"

"Another good question, Jacob. You cut right to the chase. I like you. Gospel and good news are really two sides of the same coin. The word *gospel* actually means 'good news' in Greek. The good news of the gospel of Jesus Christ is His crucifixion, death, and resurrection, at which time He took the sin of the whole world, past, present and future, upon Himself. He took the punishment for the whole world's sin and replaces our sin with His righteousness when we confess and repent of our sins. That's the good news. It's a free gift from God that we can never earn. Now, let me take it one step further and define righteousness. Righteousness is a right standing before God the Father."

Jacob made a snap decision. "Pastor Phil, I want to be baptized."

Phil gave Jacob a disbelieving stare. "Really?"

"Yes, really. Right now! Or, at least, as soon as possible." Jacob wasn't sure how he was going to keep this below his family's radar— or the seminary's radar. No one must know—for now. But he knew he was making the right decision. He knew it in his heart.

"Well, Jacob, we need to talk a bit more first." Pastor Phil said. "I need to meet some of our members for lunch in a few minutes. Care to join us? We can visit and work out the details of you getting baptized later. What do you say?"

"I say, let's go, Pastor!"

Jacob followed Pastor Phil to a small, family-owned Italian restaurant near the highway Jacob would take back to New York City later. Luigi was the portly owner everyone called Lou. He met them at the door and showed them to the private room the group usually used after church each Sunday.

Pastor Phil introduced Jacob to the group and then began introducing the assembled church members to Jacob, going around the table saying something about each of the fifteen people there. And then he came to Rachel, a radiant young woman with a smile that Jacob thought belonged on an angel's face. She wore her long dark hair in a ponytail which was hanging over her left shoulder. She appeared confident but maybe a bit shy.

"And now we come to Rachel," Pastor Phil said. "We may be losing her next month when she graduates from college. She's the daughter of a U. S. senator, so she'll probably head to Washington D. C. and probably try to run the government." Everyone chuckled.

Pastor Phil moved on to the next person at the table, but Jacob's gaze was fixed on Rachel—and she was looking back at him. And that amazed Jacob. He wasn't sure what to think or what it meant. He was aware, though, that his heart was beating differently, in a way he'd never known before. He wondered what that meant, too. He could actually hear his pulse in his ears. That was different. His breathing seemed odd, too. *What was that about?* he wondered.

"Jacob," Pastor Phil said, sounding to Jacob as though he were in another room. "Jacob," he said a little louder, bringing Jacob back into the present.

"Um, yes, Pastor Phil?"

"I said, why don't you tell them a little bit about yourself?"

"Oh, sure." Jacob told them that he was in his home stretch at the Jewish Theological Seminary in New York, where he would graduate in about six weeks; that his studies had led him to question why his Jewish brethren hadn't recognized Jesus as the Messiah; and that his further studies and cross-referencing the Gospels with the Law,

Prophets, and Psalms had convinced him that Jesus was, indeed, the long-awaited Messiah. To Jacob's surprise, the whole room exploded with applause.

Pastor Phil broke into the cheers. "And Jacob told me just before we came here that he wanted to be baptized." Once again, the room boomed with more cheers and applause.

Jacob stole a glance in Rachel's direction and saw tears on her cheeks and what looked to him like a pained expression on her face and wondered what it meant. He wanted to see her smile again, not what he saw now. Jacob's heart began to sink. His heart became buoyant again when she got up from her chair and walked around the table to give him a big hug. It startled him at first, but he accepted it gratefully. Maybe she wasn't as shy as Jacob thought.

"Your father's name isn't Laban, is it?" he whispered in her ear.

She stepped back and gave him a puzzled look.

"Sorry," he said. "Jewish joke."

Several more people came and shook his hand and congratulated him on his decision.

"Let's order lunch," Pastor Phil announced. "I'm always hungry after preaching." Everyone returned to their seats and began studying menus.

Pastor Phil brought another chair from against the wall and placed it next to his chair. "Jacob, I'd like for you to sit here next to me."

Jacob took the seat offered; and he, too, studied the menu, settling on lasagna. *Not kosher,* he thought, *Sure hope Simon Peter was right in the book of Acts about eating unclean things. Shrimp scampi next time, maybe?* He chuckled.

After lunch, Pastor Phil turned to Jacob and asked, "Are you ready?"

Jacob noticed that the good pastor had a spot of spaghetti sauce on his chin and smiled. "You'd better wipe your chin, Pastor," Jacob warned. "You have a spot of spaghetti sauce there. But I need to ask, ready for what?"

"I need to ask you a few questions before we can go forward with baptizing you," Pastor Phil said, wiping his chin with his napkin. "Since we have several of our church deacons here, I thought we could hurry the process along. Are you willing?"

"I think so. My mind is pretty much made up, though."

"I gathered that, Jacob, but we want to be sure you know what baptism means and what responsibilities you're agreeing to take on."

Jacob nodded. "Okay, let's go." He looked in Rachel's direction again. She was busy talking to the woman sitting next to her.

Pastor Phil took his only clean eating utensil, his knife, and tapped lightly on his water glass until he had everyone's attention. "Since our new friend Jacob has asked to be baptized," he announced to the group, "I feel it's important that he understand what his new responsibilities are as a Christian. Also, I want to advise him to think long and hard about what he's about to do. He'll soon be graduating from seminary to become a rabbi and it's highly unlikely that any of his Jewish brethren would be interested in having a professing Christian as their rabbi."

Pastor Phil looked directly at Jacob. "But you becoming a rabbi aside, Jacob, if you were to die tonight and were face to face with Jesus Christ and He asked you why He should let you into His Heaven, what would be your answer?"

Before answering, Jacob looked in Rachel's direction again. Her eyes were locked on his. His heart skipped a beat. "Because I believe that Jesus Christ is the Messiah."

"And . . . " Pastor Phil prompted.

"And I believe that Jesus Christ lived an exemplary life."

"I'm not trying to pick on you, Jacob, but your answers focus on what you believe—and make no mistake, your beliefs are important—but the focus must be on what Jesus did, not what we believe or what we've done. Jesus is the Fulfillment of the Law and the Prophets. He didn't live an exemplary life; He led a *perfect* life. He was crucified as the spotless Lamb of God at the Passover. Our entrance into Heaven is based upon God's grace, based upon the spotless Lamb of God taking our sins on Himself and replacing the sin taken from us with His righteousness."

"Yes," Jacob agreed, "I believe that. I cannot earn salvation."

"Good. Right answer. Now, what are you going to do about your pending graduation from seminary?"

"That's something I'm going to have to pray about. I had first thought I'd just keep it under the radar for a while, but I don't feel totally comfortable with that. It's a form of deceit. But I've studied all my life for service to my God. Now, I find myself in a sticky situation. I've discovered truth, and Jesus said in the eighth chapter of John, 'And ye shall know the truth, and the truth shall make you free.' I can now serve my God in truth."

"Yes, you'll be serving God 'in spirit and in truth,'"[1] Pastor Phil added. "We'll put your baptism on hold until you reach a final decision."

---

1   John 4:24

Jacob nodded his agreement, and the group broke up to head their various ways. He sat quietly for a couple of minutes as the others left, weighing his options.

Rachel came to him and extended her hand as he got up from his chair. "It was nice to meet you, Jacob. I hope we see each other again."

Jacob extended his hand to shake Rachel's and said, "Yes, I'd like that."

Rachel left a folded piece of paper in Jacob's hand. Once again, his heart skipped a beat as she turned to leave.

He left the restaurant and returned to his car before opening the note Rachel had left him. He felt the stirring of a thousand baby butterflies flying franticly in his midsection. *That feeling is new*, he said to himself.

"Call me, please," it read, and gave her phone number.

What could they possibly talk about, he wondered. What in the world would he have in common with the daughter of a U. S. senator? Her life must be a whirlwind of social functions and official appearances. Jacob's life consisted of study, study, study, Passover, study, study, High Holy Days, study. And if he chose to follow Christ, he would have to completely start over on his future. He wondered how it was possible to be so elated, on one hand, and so miserable on the other. He needed to pray hard on this one.

He started his car's engine and left the restaurant parking lot, turning onto the highway leading back into New York City. The mid-Sunday afternoon traffic was a bit of a distraction from his dilemma, but the burning questions needing answers were still buzzing in his mind.

He tossed and turned all that night, the questions looming larger in the dark than they had during the light of the previous day. One thing he could do, he decided that night, was to not call Rachel for a few days to see if his mind fog would lift. As much as talking with her appealed to him, he didn't need that distraction, too. He didn't know what to say, anyway.

At the end of the third week after his visit to the Assembly of God Church and three weeks until his graduation from the seminary, he had still not phoned Rachel. He had not yet accepted an assignment to a small synagogue in Connecticut. His problems were mounting, and he needed someone with whom he could talk candidly—someone who might be far enough removed from his situation to give him sound counsel. Jacob pulled out that precious piece of paper Rachel had given him and picked up the phone.

"Hello?" Rachel answered.

"Hi, Rachel. This is Jacob from church. Do you remember me?" He held his breath.

"Of course," she replied. "I was beginning to think you weren't going to call me."

"It's nearly graduation time, and things are getting pretty hectic." It wasn't an untruth.

"I'm aware of that. I'm nearly buried in finals and such myself," she agreed. "The reason I wanted you to call is because I may have a possible solution to your problem. And I've spoken with Laban since our lunch after church, and he thinks he can help you."

Wait! What? "Laban? Who's Laban?"

Rachel giggled. "Don't you remember? You asked me if my father's name is Laban. I didn't get it, and you said it was a Jewish joke. I looked it up in Genesis, and it made me laugh. I like your sense of humor. You're Jacob, and I'm Rachel. Jacob loved Rachel best. And Rachel's father was Laban. I have good news for you, Jacob. I'm an only child. There is no sister Leah. My late mother's name was Leah, though."

"Okay, I've caught up with you now. Your father's name isn't really Laban, then."

"No, his name is Paul," she said and giggled again. "I just extended your joke."

Jacob relaxed and imagined seeing her heavenly smile in his mind's eye. He laughed. "Got me good, didn't you?"

"I just wanted to make you laugh like I laughed when I discovered the significance of Laban and Rachel . . . and now Jacob."

"Thank you, Rachel. I've needed some humor to lighten this burden I've been carrying. I've been assigned to a small synagogue in Connecticut, which I haven't accepted yet. I have to start my whole life plan over."

"It may not be as hard as you think," she said. "Laban suggests you graduate from seminary, and then he can help you get a commission in the army as a chaplain. That way, you can serve your Jewish brothers as well as your Christian brothers. What do you think?"

"I never imagined myself in the military, but it's certainly a perfect solution." Jacob said. He also thought—since she had asked what he thought—that she was brilliant *and* beautiful.

"I hoped you'd see the wisdom in this. Daddy—that's Laban to you—and I will be in New York next week. He wants to meet you . . . and I'd like to see you again, too. We'll be taking you to dinner. Can you arrange to meet us?"

Jacob stammered something about wild horses, which he knew nothing about but promised they wouldn't keep him away.

"Great," Rachel said. "I can't wait to see you again, Jacob."

Jacob couldn't wait either.

Just two weeks after Jacob graduated from seminary, he was heading back to the little white church and Pastor Phil. And this Sunday was *the* Sunday of his baptism. The plus was that he would see Rachel and Paul, whom he and Rachel called "Laban" between themselves. He had been chatting with her almost daily by phone since their luncheon with "Laban." Jacob chuckled to himself every time "Laban" was mentioned, the innocent joke continued.

Arriving early, Jacob pulled into the gravel parking lot. He hurriedly jumped out of his car, anxious for his moment to arrive. He had been looking forward to this day ever since he first announced his desire for baptism. He bounded up the four steps and into the church, meeting Walter, one of the deacons he had met during his first after-church get-together for lunch.

"Hi, Jacob," Walter greeted. "Ready for your big day?"

"Absolutely," Jacob replied. "Do you know where I can find Pastor Phil? He asked me to arrive early."

"I think you'll find him in the sanctuary."

Jacob thanked him and headed in that direction, finding the pastor down in front wearing a white robe. On his way to the front of the church, Jacob noticed that the curtain he remembered hanging behind the pulpit had been opened, revealing an empty space about six feet long and five feet wide and having a glass front to a four-foot-deep tank, holding back the water. *That must be the place,* Jacob thought.

Pastor Phil spotted Jacob heading his way and sent him a huge smile of greeting. "Let's get you ready, Jacob."

The pastor explained the details of what was going to happen and then gave him a package. "There's a white robe, like mine, in this package," he said. "I want you to go into the men's room and change into this robe. Bring your clothes back here with you, and we'll put them outside the baptismal pool for you to get back into after you dry off. There are already towels there for us to get dry. We're going to do your baptism first thing. I'm going to ask you several questions, and you will answer them honestly. After that, I will place one of my hands on the back of your head and one hand on your back. I'll lean you back beneath the water and say, 'I baptize you in the name of the Father, and the Son, and the Holy Spirit,' and bring you back up. There's already a towel up there for you to wipe your face. After you dry your face, I'll introduce you to the church as our newest brother baptized in Jesus Christ. Now, I want you to go and change into your robe and come back down here and sit on the front row. I'll tell you when to come forward once we get started. Any questions?"

Jacob shook his head "no" and started toward the men's room. He changed from his suit and tie into the free-flowing white robe that looked to Jacob like the garb some Middle Eastern men wear every day and made his way back to the front of the church sanctuary. He took a seat on the front row, folded his hands in his lap, and waited. He watched Pastor Phil putter around behind the pulpit for a few minutes, greet a few people who came forward to pay their respects, and then go to the back of the church. Then Jacob waited some more until the piano player began playing praise music he'd heard during his last visit here some weeks back, and the congregation began singing.

They sang three praise songs in succession. Then, during the last song, an odd thing happened. Pastor Phil came back without wearing the white robe as before. Jacob wrinkled his brow.

The pastor walked up the two steps to the pulpit and smiled broadly at his congregation. "Good morning, friends," he said. "Today is a very special day for the body of Christ because we are going to witness the baptism of our new friend Jacob. And Jacob doesn't know it yet, but we've had a little change of plans." He looked at Jacob with a smile.

Jacob squirmed, not knowing where this was headed. He didn't think Christians sacrificed Jews. He wondered if he should stand up and testify that he was a Christian now!

Pastor Phil turned to the baptismal pool and called out, "Paul."

Paul stepped down the steps and into the pool wearing the white robe Pastor Phil had worn before. The congregation applauded loudly, and Paul raised his hand in a wave.

"What some of you don't know," Pastor Phil continued, "is that the senator from the great state of Missouri is an ordained minister and served as such before he got dragged, kicking and screaming, into public service. And of course, you all know that he's also the father of our own Rachel, who has attended church here ever since she's been a student in the college down the road. Do you have anything to add, Paul?"

"Yes, I do," Paul said. "And I won't say anything political." The congregation clapped and cheered loudly. Paul raised his hand again to quiet the crowd. "Jacob, will you join me in the baptismal pool, please?

Jacob got up and moved toward the door to the pool, opened it, and joined Paul in the pool.

"It seems that my darling daughter has taken a shine to young Jacob, and she has never actually demanded that I meet any young man before this one," continued Paul. "Since she was so insistent about my meeting him, I figured I needed to check this thing out. I now understand why she's taken with him. He has a keen wit and a wonderful sense of humor. When Rachel first met Jacob, he joked by asking if her father's name is Laban; and my nickname ever since has been—you guessed it—Laban. In order to fully understand his joke, you must read the book of Genesis, beginning at the twenty-ninth chapter."

Jacob hoped Paul's speech wasn't going to last much longer because the water was not as warm as he would have liked.

"Rachel told me that Jacob was the bravest person she's ever met. He was abandoning everything he's ever known to follow Jesus Christ. She's impressed with him; and when Rachel asked me if I would baptize him, I cleared it with Pastor Phil, since it's his jurisdiction. And here we are." Turning his attention to Jacob he said, "Are you ready, Jacob? It will be my honor to baptize you!"

Jacob nodded, totally taken by surprise by the whole thing. He had trouble keeping his emotions in check.

Paul baptized Jacob, who was grateful that he was not the first Jew to be sacrificed by this church. Paul handed him the towel for him to wipe his face dry and said, "There's one more thing I want to tell you about young Jacob. On the nineteenth of next month, he will be leaving for U. S. Army 'charm school,' otherwise known as OCS or Officer Candidate School. After he graduates OCS, he will be commissioned as a U. S. Army captain in the Chaplain Corps, since he has recently been ordained as a rabbi. Because of his advanced education and a few political favors, he will skip second and first lieutenant. Now, will you please welcome our newest addition to the body of Christ: Jacob. I know you'll love him as much as Rachel and I already do."

Jacob searched the congregation for Rachel. He found her with tears streaming down her face, wearing the same pained expression he'd seen once before. *I hope that's a look of joy*, he thought. And then it struck him. Paul had said "love him as much as Rachel and I do." *Does that mean Rachel loves me?* he wondered. Those blasted baby butterflies came back to his mid-section with a vengeance as he gazed at her lovely, tear-stained face.

CHAPTER 6
JULES NEEDS HELP

After Julie returned home from the hospital, she spent the better part of three days doing nothing but caring for little Eric, fuming about Matt, and thinking about Cathy's parting words. Some of the things she had said were still stinging, but the part about Cath not being able to have children bothered her the most.

"I didn't know," Julie said aloud to no one. "How could I have known? And if I had known, would I still have aborted *my* baby?"

Julie hadn't heard from her mother since she had driven Julie home from the hospital, mostly in silence. *Just as well,* Julie thought. *I don't need her lectures.* But Julie's mind kept drifting back to her old friend. Cathy had truly tried to be a friend and help in her time of need. She watched little Eric play with his toy trucks and thought, *How could I have been so cold and self-centered? I was acting just like my mother would. I hate it when she acts like the queen of the universe, when every bad thing that happens is a sinister plot against her alone.*

Not knowing what she was going to say or even if she would say anything at all if Cathy answered, Julie picked up her phone and called her friend. She let the phone ring six times and was about to hang up when Cathy answered.

"Hello?" she said.

"Um, uh, this is Julie, Cath."

"Oh! Jules, I'm so glad you phoned. I thought I'd lost you for good."

"Well, uh, I've thought a lot about what you said to me in the hospital, and, uh, I'm sorry. I didn't know you weren't able to have kids. If I had known, I'm not sure I would have done anything different; but I wanted you to know that I truly am sorry. When I look at my little Eric, I don't know what I'd do without him. I'm trying to imagine how I'd feel if I hadn't been able to have him, and I'm drawing a blank."

"That's okay. Apology accepted."

"Something else I want you to know is that I realized that I was acting just like my mom, and I certainly don't want to be the 'Pitiful Pearl' she is. I don't want to sound like I'm blaming her, but we do learn most of how to behave in life from our parents."

"Well, you can break the pattern, but you'll need help."

"I'm asking for your help, Cath! I need your help!"

"Yes, I absolutely will help you, but you'll need more than just my help, Jules."

"I figured you'd say that, but I've gotten to the point that I'm ready for His help, too. I made a mess of things, and my efforts haven't been too successful."

"We'll get together soon, Jules."

"Probably the sooner, the better," Julie said.

The more Julie thought about the way Matt had treated her—the sheer lack of any compassion, the rudeness, and his utter disdain for her—the angrier she got. In fact, she was seething mad. She wanted to deal with him. Get back at him. Make him hurt, just the way he made her hurt, feel cheap, and, well, dirty. But how to do it?

She'd confronted him at his watering hole, and that had backfired. He and his friends had just laughed at her. The whole situation had escalated from one stupid night that she wished she could undo—or, at least, forget. He denied everything. *Just like a lawyer,* she thought. She was mad enough to shoot, stab, poison, run over him with her car, push him over a cliff, throw him in front of a bus—you name it. She was ready to make him pay. But she couldn't get caught. She had little Eric to think about. It had to be something that no one must ever suspect that she had done. No one must ever know.

Julie sighed. She knew she'd never go through with it. It excited her to think about it, though. Something about her thoughts about Matt felt wrong—something she couldn't quite put her finger on. Cath said she needed to forgive Matt and move on. But Julie didn't think she could ever forget it. What she'd gone through for one night of stupidity was too much to forget. And then to kill her baby . . .

She began to cry. She thought her mother's advice to get an abortion was the right thing to do at the time; but now, she wasn't so sure. She was having feelings about it she couldn't explain. She had lost her baby—on purpose.

Julie walked over to little Eric playing with his trucks, picked him up, and held him tight. "I love you sooooo much, little man," she said to him. He squirmed to get down and play with his trucks again.

How in the world, she thought, *could such a cute, sweet person like little Eric grow into a self-centered creep like Matt?*

———————————.✦.———

Julie and Cathy were having coffee at Cathy's apartment. Little Eric was sitting in front of Julie's television playing with his trucks as the morning news blared from the TV. Julie was, once again, complaining endlessly about what Matt had done to her.

"Jules," Cathy began, "what Matt did was wrong, yes. What you did was equally wrong. All this hate raging in you isn't hurting Matt one bit. He doesn't care. It is, however, hurting you. I've heard you going on and on about what Matt did for weeks. It's time to let it go."

"Oh, sure, Cath, it's easy for you to say. You're not the one who went through what he put me through."

"You're right. I didn't go through it, but the essential truth is that I cannot imagine putting myself in that situation in the first place. You're reaping the crop that you planted. You're familiar with God's law of sowing and reaping, aren't you?

"I'm not a farmer! What do I care about farming?"

"God's law of sowing and reaping deals with farming, yes, but the same law applies to everything in life. If you plant a kernel of corn, in due time, you will receive a crop of two or three hundred kernels from every one you planted. If we lie, we're lied about and lied to—we reap the crop we've sown. If we cheat, we're cheated—we reap the crop we've sown. If we steal, we're stolen from—we reap the crop we've sown. But if we are generous, we receive generosity—we reap the crop we've sown. If we love our neighbor like Jesus told us to, we are loved in return. We reap the crop we've sown—one, two, three hundred times over."

"I did love my neighbor, and look what it got me!" Julie protested.

"No, Julie, don't confuse love with lust. You committed adultery, cheated on your husband, and look at what it got you. You're reaping the crop you've sown."

Julie's head suddenly snapped to look at the television screen when the announcer said something which snagged her attention. Her mouth dropped, and her eyes got wide. "Look, Cath!" she said. "That's a picture of Matt on the TV!"

Cathy looked at the TV screen and saw a picture of a nice-looking man in a police mug shot. The announcer said that Matt, a prominent lawyer, had been arrested for drunk driving, leaving the scene of an accident and killing two teenagers while driving drunk.

"Wow," Julie said in a hushed tone, "You really do reap what you sow."

Cathy looked across the table at her friend and said, "I know you wanted to pinch Matt's head off, but, Jules, those of us who follow Jesus have to remember what God's Word says about getting even. It's in Romans twelve: 'Vengeance is mine; I will repay, saith the Lord.'"

"Couldn't happen to a nicer guy," Julie said.

"Maybe you should replace your last statement with 'I forgive you, Matt,'" Cathy said quietly. "Maybe you could pray for Matt. Maybe you could let go of this hatred you have for him and get on with your life. Sowing a negative attitude will only reap a crop of more negativity. Accept responsibility for your own actions, confess and ask God for forgiveness, and drive on. You're just making yourself miserable."

Julie's eyes began to tear. "What can I do, Cath? I'm just so angry."

"I get that, and I think you need to forgive yourself first."

Julie began crying. "Cath! I murdered my baby. How can I ever be forgiven for that?"

Cathy got up from her chair and walked around the table to put her arm around her friend. "Jules, you're probably not going to like this, but I'm going to quote what the Bible says in 1 John 1:9: 'If we confess our sins, he is faithful and just to forgive us our sins, and to cleanse us from all unrighteousness.' I like to change that verse a bit and make it personal. I like to say, 'If I confess *my* sins, Jesus Christ is faithful and just to forgive *my* sins and cleanse *me* from all unrighteousness.' That verse applies to you as well as me."

"Oh, Cath, I wish I could believe that."

"Let me ask you, Jules, how are things going for you right now?"

"Horrible! I could just scream," Julie answered.

"Then, it seems to me that you should be looking for a way to make some changes, right?"

"Yes, but I don't know if I'm ready for all that Christian stuff you keep spouting."

"You only have two choices, Jules. It's either what you call 'all that Christian stuff' or what you've been doing all your life. Since what you've been doing doesn't seem to be working too well, you need to make a decision. And it's your move. Jesus loves you, and He wants to help you—but you have to let Him. He's a Gentleman and won't step in unless you ask."

"I don't know if I can do it, Cath. It seems so foreign to me. Isn't there some way to ease into it?"

"When you married Eric, did you make a commitment; or did you look for some way to 'ease into it'?"

"But I knew Eric, and I only know *about* Jesus. And I don't know very much about Him at that."

Cathy smiled. "That's an easy fix. Just pick up the Bible I gave you and read the Gospel according to John. I'll find it for you. I'll even sit down and read with you. Then re-read it. Pray for guidance and insight every time you read. Pretty soon, you'll not only know Him, but you'll fall in love with Him."

"Fall in love with Him? That sounds silly."

"It probably does now; but if you ask Jesus to step in, you'll soon see for yourself."

"Okay, but what can we do right now? I feel miserable."

Cathy broke into a huge grin. "Well, Jules, my beloved friend, it's time you and I get on our knees and pray together, okay?"

CHAPTER 7
MATT TAKES A DIVE

Matt sat on his usual bar stool studying himself in the mirror mounted behind the bar. He was nearly plastered. His drinking too much was becoming a habit—a habit he didn't like much but one he kept at, nonetheless. And it was beginning to have a negative impact on his law practice. He would turn thirty in a couple of months and had dreamed of becoming a partner before he reached that age. That was definitely not in the cards, since the managing partner of his firm had been hounding him about his lack of bringing in new business. Not to mention his disdain of Matt's reputation for chasing every skirt within his field of vision.

"Matt," his boss said to him earlier that day, "you're a smart guy. We hired you because of your outgoing personality, your law school GPA, and your LSAT score. We all agreed that you had the potential to become a huge asset to the firm. You're letting us down. I've seen lots of smart but incompetent lawyers who had potential make it all the way to Washington D.C. while being too lazy to achieve much. Politics pays well for those who don't have the moxie to accomplish much." His boss' "incompetent" crack would have stung even more if Matt hadn't had such a hangover.

Charlie, the bartender arrived to see if Matt needed another drink.

"No, Charlie, I think I need to slow down a bit. My boss is on my case about the booze and the 'Big Boss' hates my pursuit of the ladies. I need a change."

Charlie chuckled. "Well, I think there are a few ladies around that might want to thank your boss in that case."

Matt staggered to his feet, knocking over the barstool. "Just what is that supposed to mean?"

Charlie raised his hands defensively. "Hey now, it was just a joke. Don't go taking it personally."

"'Don't' you tell me what to do!" Matt screamed. He staggered from the bar, got in his 1955 Cadillac Coupe de Ville, fumbled for his keys, started the engine and sped away from his favorite bar. A few blocks later, he sped through a red light at twenty-five miles per hour above the posted thirty mile per hour speed limit and T-boned a small Nash Metropolitan carrying two teenage girls. The Nash rolled over sideways several times by the impact, finally coming to rest on its crushed top.

Matt panicked and fled. The radiator of the Cadillac had been severely damaged by the wreck and gushed coolant for six blocks until the engine locked-up and quit. Matt tried to exit his car but the driver door wouldn't open because of the crash. He was in no condition to walk anyhow. He heard emergency vehicle sirens in the distance. It didn't take long for the police to find him with the Cadillac's engine spewing steam like it was. The police arrested him for driving while intoxicated and leaving the scene of an accident. It was only when Matt was charged with their deaths that he learned that the two girls in the Nash had been pronounced dead at the scene.

———————————— ·✦· ——

Six lawyers filed into the law firm's conference room. The seventh, the managing partner, last to enter, closed the door behind himself.

"I've asked you here today to discuss what we, as a law firm, will do about one of our lawyers who has recently been arrested for killing two teenage girls in an auto accident, driving intoxicated and leaving the scene of an accident. You are all partners, and we, as a group, will decide the official stance of the firm. Since we are primarily a divorce and injury law firm, we don't actually have anyone on staff who is a qualified trial lawyer for a case of this nature." He looked around the room to get a feel for the general mood of the group, but they were each wearing a poker face. "Does anyone have any questions so far?"

A female partner asked, "What are his chances for a plea deal?"

The managing partner cleared his throat and continued, "Matt was tanked, as usual, and had caused a scene at the bar he left. There are no less than a half-dozen witnesses to the bar incident leading up to the auto accident. Their stories are all pretty much the same. It's really hard to say what his chances are, but the court of public opinion has pretty much crucified him for killing two teenagers while he was inebriated."

"What are you thinking, boss?" another partner asked.

"I'm going to keep that to myself, for now," he said. "I'm going to have each of you take a slip of paper, and we'll have a secret ballot. I will not vote, except to break a tie. Your yes vote indicates that you think we, as a firm, should try to find Matt a good defense attorney. Your no vote says you think we should throw him in front of the oncoming train and let him find his own lawyer or hope for a decent public defender, distancing ourselves from him." He passed slips of paper to each of them to record their votes.

Each partner recorded his or her vote, folded the slip of paper, and passed their vote to the managing partner who opened each slip and read each vote aloud.

"It's unanimous," he announced. "Matt is on his own. Meeting adjourned. And just for the record, my vote would have been identical to all of yours."

CHAPTER 8
CATHY GETS A SURPRISE

Cathy woke up on Saturday morning wondering what she would do for the day. She wasn't in any big hurry to get out of bed, so she just stretched and lay there, enjoying the laziness of it all. She began her morning worship time in prayer without ever setting foot on the floor. As she prayed for Jules, God the Holy Spirit gave her an idea. She thought, *Thanks, Lord. I'll do just that.* She finished her prayer and worship time, got out of bed, and picked up her telephone and dialed. Jules answered.

"Hey, Julie, let's you and me drive into downtown Cheyenne and do some shopping. I'll bet you could use some time out of the house."

"I'd like that. Do you think I should take little E, or should I get a sitter? I could call Mom and see if she'll watch him for a while. Are you coming here, or am I coming to get you?"

It was pretty obvious to Cathy that Julie was excited about the proposed outing, since Jules didn't let Cathy answer any of her questions before launching into the next one.

"I'll come to get you; and if your mom will watch Eric, we'll drive to your mom's house to drop him off."

"Great," Jules said. "Come and get me in an hour."

Cathy arrived about fifteen minutes late, apologizing that she just couldn't make up her mind about which shoes, skirt, or blouse to wear. Jules smiled knowingly, as though she may have had the same problem.

The two girls and Eric piled into Cathy's old Chevy and headed for Julie's mom's house about ten minutes away to drop Eric.

Julie's mom, with no hair out of place, seemed pleased to see her grandson.

"We won't be too long," reassured Cathy. "Jules and I haven't gone shopping together in ages. We'll be back soon."

Off they went, chatting like old times. They went into several downtown stores, browsed around, and bought nothing.

"Cath," Julie said when they got back to the car, "I've been thinking a lot about what you said about me forgiving Matt. The more I think about it and the more I read the words of Jesus in the red letters of the Bible you gave me, the more I know you're right."

Cathy felt her heart melting for her friend. "Oh, Jules, that's wonderful news. You won't regret making that decision."

"Wait, Cath, there's more. I want to visit him in jail and tell him to his face."

Cathy felt her jaw drop, not knowing what to say.

"I made a few phone calls and found out that he's being held in the Laramie County Jail, and I can visit him after 1 p.m. today. I didn't want to go alone, and I hoped you'd go with me."

Cathy wasn't sure she was ready for what was in front of her, but she made the snap decision that she *must* accompany her friend on her mission. She couldn't back out now, since it was her idea in the first place for Julie to forgive and forget. "Sure, Jules. I can do nothing less than support you." Cathy looked at her watch and said, "We have time to grab some lunch first."

They drove to the area of the jail and found a diner. Going inside, they found an empty booth, sat down, and ordered a burger and a small bottle of Coke apiece. They ate mostly in silence. Cathy supposed the silence was largely because they were both nervous about going into the jail, a new experience for both of them.

From the diner, the two girls walked the short distance to the jail and stopped in front before going inside. They looked at each other, Cathy wishing Julie would change her mind.

"Well, here goes," Julie said as she stepped toward the entrance.

After entering, they found an officer at a desk with three stripes on the sleeve of his shirt. Julie told the officer that she wanted to see one of the prisoners and give his name.

"Does he know you're coming?" the officer asked.

"No," Julie said. "I called to find out where he was being held and what time I could visit is all."

"What's your name?" he asked. Julie told him. "Do you both want to see him?" asked the officer.

"Can we both see him?" Julie wanted to know.

The officer nodded and asked Cathy her name. He made a phone call to see if they could visit with him.

The officer hung up the phone and directed them to a door down the hall to the left of the entryway. Someone would meet them there in a couple of minutes. They would be searched for weapons and anything prisoners were not allowed to have. Then they would be taken to a visiting room, where the prisoner would be waiting for them behind a wire mesh barrier for their safety.

The girls walked hesitantly down the long, dark hallway and waited. When someone opened the heavy steel door, it startled them both. Cathy wanted to run.

Another officer with three stripes on the sleeve of his shirt said to them, "Step inside, please." They did without a word. The officer closed the steel door with a loud clang, which made Cathy jump again. He locked the door behind them and stepped around the girls, saying, "Follow me, please."

The officer led them down another long, dark hallway. He opened a door at the end and motioned the girls to enter. Inside was a large woman officer with three stripes on her shirt, who said, "Come in ladies."

They entered, looking at each other with faces which silently screamed, *what have we gotten ourselves into?*

"Now, ladies," the female officer began, "I'm going to be searching you before you can see the prisoner. I will ask you first if you have any contraband items like knives, guns, razors, illegal drugs, or anything else which might be used to harm either prisoners or guards. If you do, please give them up now and save everyone, especially yourselves, a load of trouble. If we find any of those items after I've given you the opportunity to give them up freely, it will be most unpleasant to be you, understand?"

Both girls nodded and swallowed hard.

The female officer frisked both girls and found nothing. "You will not be allowed to take your purses into the visiting room. Put your purses into one of the lockers along the back wall, remove the key from the lock in which your purse is located, and remember the number of the locker. You will place the key on a nail with the corresponding number hanging outside the visiting room. You will retrieve your key after your visit, come back here to get your purse, and then you may leave." She went to the door, opened it, and said, "Roscoe, they're clean."

The girls left the female officer behind and followed Roscoe again to the visiting room where, as promised, were nails with numbers painted above them for the girls to hang their keys. Roscoe unlocked another heavy steel door, which led to the visiting room. Upon entering the visiting room, they found Matt, unshaven and looking like a whipped dog sitting behind the mesh screen.

When Matt saw his visitors he said, "Well, well, well. The cute little Julie chick. Come to gloat, did you?"

"No, Matt. I've come to forgive you for everything that happened."

"Forgive me? You had just as much to do with it as I did, girlie."

"Yes, I did. It took my friend, Cathy, here to help me come to grips with all this. I'm a Christian now, and I felt it necessary to forgive you face to face. I hated you for the cowardly way you just snuck away without a word or even a note. And then when I wound up pregnant with your baby and you denied everything, I wanted to hurt you any way I could. I had an abortion. I murdered my baby . . . your baby . . . our baby. It wasn't that poor baby's fault. The baby didn't do anything to deserve death. It was you and me, but the baby paid the price. Cathy kept telling me to forgive myself and you for the whole mess. She kept saying everyone reaps what they sow. Well, I'm sowing forgiveness, and I wanted you to know it."

"Well, you can keep your goody-two-shoes forgiveness. I don't need it. And don't come around here anymore."

"Don't worry, Matt. I won't come back. The forgiveness you need is the forgiveness of Jesus Christ."

"Get out! Get out!" Matt screamed, as the guard behind him grabbed him by both arms from behind and ushered him toward the door to go back to his cell. Roscoe opened the exit door when he heard Matt yelling; and the girls exited the visiting room, taking their keys off the nails and going to get their purses. Cathy felt like she couldn't get out of there fast enough.

As the girls left the jail building, Cathy said, "I'm thrilled you're admitting to being a Christian, Jules, but I'm not too sure we're ready to launch into a prison ministry."

————————————.✦⁺————

The drive back to Julie's mom's house was mostly in silence. The jail experience had stressed and terrified them both. Cathy spoke first, "I never knew what jail was like. I'm not sure what I expected, but I didn't expect *that*!"

Julie nodded her head in agreement.

"It took a lot of courage for you, a new Christian, to do what you did," Cathy continued. "You showed Matt the love of Jesus, just like he told us to do. You planted a seed. That seed may not grow, at least not right away, but it's God the Holy Spirit who makes those things happen, not us. I'm proud of you Jules, and I can imagine Jesus smiling at your efforts."

Cathy pulled into the driveway of Julie's mom's house, and Julie jumped out of the car to get her son.

Julie was gone for nearly five minutes before she appeared at the door and motioned Cathy inside. Cathy turned off her car engine and went to the door, where a shocked-looking Julie was still standing. "You're not going to believe this," Julie whispered as Cathy passed by.

"Hello, Catherine," Julie's mom said, "it's nice to see you again, and I truly wish you'd start calling me Barb."

Cathy smiled at her invitation and said, "Okay . . . Barb." Her pleasant attitude and tone of voice was totally out of character from anything Cathy had remembered from before. Cathy had just assumed that she was treated the old way because Cathy's father was a black man. This was new and unexpected.

"Girls, please sit down because I have a story to tell you and then a proposal to make for the both of you."

Cath and Jules looked at one another and took a cautious seat at the table where Barb was seated. Then the girls looked at each other again as if to say an unspoken *What's this?*

"Julie," Barb began, looking at her daughter, "your father was a very good man. He was every insurance salesman's dream because he believed in having enough insurance to take care of anything life threw at him. As an example, he took out an insurance policy on our mortgage so that if he were to die suddenly, like he did, the policy would pay off the entire mortgage and leave you and me with a house free and clear. In retrospect, I'm grateful for his foresight. He also had enough life insurance to provide for me for the rest of my life. But he also had an insurance policy in the amount of twenty-five thousand dollars earmarked for his only child—you. When he died, I put the principal amount into an interest-bearing account, which has been increasing in value ever since your father passed away. But I'll get back to that later."

She paused and took a sip of the hot tea she had sitting in front of her. "I want to go back to the time when your father was away fighting in World War II. You were very small when he left, and I resented him being gone. Of course, his being gone wasn't his fault but I was desperately lonely and made a terrible mistake. My mistake was the same mistake you made, with the same result. I said to myself, 'No one will ever know,' which was a lie because *I* knew. I've known ever since, and I've hated myself for it. You don't have any siblings because of the botched abortion, which left me unable to have more children but almost made you an orphan and your dad a widower. I've given of my mistake and the same mistake made by you a great deal of thought—and tears—and I've come to the conclusion that you should be able to go to Germany to be with your husband. I couldn't do it, but *you can!* You have plenty of money to do it with the money your dad set aside for you, and you should be with him. Eric is a good boy, and I can tell by the way he looks at you that he loves you dearly."

Julie burst into tears. "Oh, Mama, I didn't know, but I understand because that's exactly what I went through."

Turning to Cathy, Barb said, "I'm grateful for you, Cathy. I didn't have a friend during my troubles like you are to Julie. You girls are like sisters. One white sister and one brown sister but sisters nonetheless. I envy you both and, if you want, I'm going to pay your way to go and help her with setting up her new life. Julie's dad left me plenty and made sure I'd have enough money to never run out."

Cathy's jaw dropped. "I don't know what to say."

"Well, you needn't say anything. If we're going to get this thing done, we've got a lot of work to do. Passports, travel arrangements, putting your lives on hold here in Cheyenne, and probably a bunch of things none of us even know about yet."

CHAPTER 9
CAL'S MORNING AFTER

Cal returned to his barracks in the late afternoon of his third day away. He looked much calmer and more refreshed than when Eric had seen him last.

"I've been worried about you, pal. Where have you been?" Eric wanted to know.

"Recharging my batteries," was all Cal would say in front of the other soldiers. "Have you had chow?"

"No," Eric replied, "I've been worried about you, so I haven't eaten much the last few days you've been gone. Let's go. I'm suddenly hungry."

The two friends left the barracks and hurried toward the mess hall before they closed for the evening.

"Where have you been, Cal?" Eric asked as they got in line.

"The chaplain arranged for me to get a seventy-two-hour pass to help me get my head together after I got Darlene's letter."

"You mean the 'Jew boy' chaplain helped you? That's hard for me to swallow."

Cal stopped in his tracks. Eric followed suit and turned toward Cal, looking puzzled.

"Eric," Cal scolded softly, "yes, the chaplain is trained as a Jewish rabbi. But you and the rest of the world needs to know that he is a good and decent man who genuinely wants to help the soldiers of this command. And for that matter, I believe he'd help the soldiers of any command—or any organization to which he's assigned. There is more to him than you or anyone else here knows. And something you don't know, Eric, is that the chaplain is actually a Christian."

"Sorry, Cal. I didn't mean to offend you."

"Please don't be so quick to judge those you don't know. He helped me a lot."

"Okay, okay. I get it. But you still haven't told me where you've been."

"I checked into a hotel in town. I cried; I prayed; I read my Bible. I cried some more, prayed some more, and read my Bible some more. And slowly, after much crying, praying, and Bible study, the Lord healed my heart enough to forgive Darlene and move on with my life. God revealed some pretty neat things to me in my Bible study. I've probably read the verses He highlighted to me fifty times, but I missed the significance. In Ecclesiastes 7:8, he says 'Better is the end of a thing than the beginning thereof.' Cool, huh?"

"Well, I guess it's cool, but I really don't understand how it applies to you."

"It means, my friend, that God has always had a plan for my life, and I have to be patient enough to find out His best for me. It also means He knew this would be the end of Darlene and me from the very beginning. Falling in love with her gave me the experience of what it feels like to truly love someone else. I'll know it when it happens again—and it will happen again. Now it's up to me to be patient and wait on the Lord."

At morning roll call, two days after Cal's return, his platoon sergeant gave him a note directing him to report, first thing, to the chaplain's office, saying, "Captain Jew wants to talk to you." Then he snickered.

Cal just nodded his head without saying anything about the rudeness of the sergeant's remark. It would serve no useful purpose, and Cal knew that well.

Cal hurried toward the base chapel, wondering what was on the chaplain's mind. He hadn't given much thought to what the chaplain had said about wanting to talk to him again, but he was glad for the opportunity to visit with him again.

As he entered the chapel, he heard soft talking and thought the chaplain must be in his office with someone or on the phone. He walked into the reception area. No receptionist.

Probably too early for her, Cal thought.

He popped his head through the chaplain's office door and found the office empty. But he still heard soft talking, so he headed for the worship chapel. There was the chaplain, kneeling on the kneeling pads at the front, hands raised in worshipful praise. The scene filled Cal's heart with joy. He quietly took a seat in the rear of the chapel and waited for the chaplain to finish. Cal's respect for this man grew with each meeting.

After several minutes more of soft talking, the chaplain's voice rose as he said, "'Hear, O Israel, the Lord our God is one Lord: and thou shalt love the Lord your God with all thine heart, and with all thy soul and with all thy might.'2 Amen." And the chaplain rose to his feet, turned and headed for the door, spotting Cal, sitting quietly in the back of the chapel.

"Welcome, my friend," Jacob said, smiling. "I'm glad you got here so early."

"Good morning, Chaplain. I got word you wanted to see me."

"Yes, I do. Let's go into my office and chat for a while. I've arranged for you to be away from your duties today—and maybe from now on, depending on what we decide to do." Jacob smiled and winked. Cal had no idea where this was heading, but he had at least been warned that this chat was in his future.

Jacob gestured to the chair Cal had occupied the last time he was in this office and, instead of the chaplain going behind his desk, he took the other seat in front of his desk. Cal felt more relaxed by the chaplain sitting on the same side of the desk as he was.

"The reason I wanted to visit with you, Cal, is because I need a chaplain's assistant, and I think you're just the right man for the job." The chaplain was quiet for nearly a minute before speaking again. He was waiting for the shock on Cal's face to fade. "What do you think?"

A multitude of questions were buzzing through Cal's head, so many questions he was having trouble focusing on just one. "What about . . . what about . . . what about my MOS?" he finally managed to say.

"Your military occupational specialty is just an administrative function that can be fixed with little trouble," Jacob said. "You can type, can't you?"

---

2   Deuteronomy 6:4

"Yes, my nana made me take it in school," Cal replied. "But I'm not very fast. I can only do about twenty-five or thirty words a minute."

"That's good enough. Are you interested in taking the job, Cal?"

The puzzled, worried expression on Cal's face vanished and was replaced by a huge smile and sheer joy. "Yes, I am . . . but I have so many questions . . ."

"I understand. Let me ask you. What is your favorite kind of pie?"

"Cherry!" Cal answered emphatically, but that quickly changed to puzzlement. "Why?"

"Okay, then, let's say you have a cherry pie sitting in front of you, and it's all just for you. Can you eat the whole thing in just one bite?"

Cal smiled and said, "Nana says I could, but she's exaggerating some. I'd rather eat it slow and enjoy it."

"Well, then, I'd like for you to approach your questions and new job the same way as you'd approach eating that cherry pie: eat it slow and enjoy it."

"Okay, I get it. But let me ask you this: why don't you already have an assistant now?"

"Before I arrived here, the former chaplain's assistant found out that I was of Jewish heritage and asked for an immediate transfer. He was gone the next day. The job has been vacant ever since. I was told that if I wanted an assistant, I needed to find my own; and the powers that be would make it happen. Politics, you know. Now, I want you to understand, there may be some pushback in this; but I don't want you to worry about that. Let me fight those battles. I have my own 'pushback' up my sleeve. You just do the best job you can, and everything will be fine. Okay?"

Cal's face darkened again. "Is the pushback because I'm black?"

"No, Cal. The pushback is because I'm Jewish. They don't even know about you yet, but they soon will." Jacob reached over to his desk and picked up a book, which he handed to Cal. "This is the sergeant's manual, which I'd like for you to study before the next exam cycle next month. I want my new chaplain's assistant to be promoted to sergeant."

The smile returned to Cal's face as his eyes widened, and he whispered an almost reverent sounding, "Sergeant?"

Colonel Harkrider was fuming mad, mostly at himself for making promises to that Jewish chaplain he never thought he'd have to fulfill. He'd promised the chaplain that he'd approve anyone he could find who would serve as his chaplain's assistant, certain he'd find no one willing. He promised to make sure anyone who took the job would be eligible for the sergeant's exam for the next cycle. He promised that the one taking the sergeant's exam from the chaplain's office would be promoted to sergeant. "Why did I ever make those promises?" he said aloud to no one.

It seemed to the colonel that the chaplain was doing everything he could just to get under his skin. So, what does the chaplain do? He gets a black kid to take the job. A black kid! Now what was he going to do? He had to keep his word. Or did he? As a colonel, he could surely come up with something to nix the whole shebang.

A knock at his office door brought him back from his thoughts. "Come," he said. His aide stuck his head through the door, "Colonel, Lieutenant General Short on the line for you, sir."

"What in the world does he want?" the colonel said under his breath. He picked up his phone and answered with a false pleasantry, "To what do I owe this honor, General Short?"

"Colonel, I just got off the phone with President Eisenhower, and I want to make sure we are all on the same page as far as the chaplain assigned to your command is concerned. You know how Ike was disturbed after he toured the Nazi concentration and death camps at the end of World War II. He was sickened. Let's make sure your Jewish chaplain gets everything he needs to do his job."

"Absolutely, General. I was just sitting here thinking about how I might serve him better just as you called," the colonel lied.

"That's a good thing, Colonel, because the wife of your chaplain is the only daughter of a United States senator."

"Yes, sir!" the colonel said as he placed the phone back on its cradle. He rolled his eyes. "Sure, I will," the colonel said. "They call me 'Horrible Harkrider' for a reason. No one will ever know why it all fell apart."

CHAPTER 10
ERIC AND CAL CHAT

The evening after Cal's meeting with the chaplain, Eric and Cal were in their barracks alone. Their two roommates were out. Cal was reading his Bible. Eric looked up from the book Cal had given him to read about Jesus' life and studied Cal for several quiet minutes. *Cal is the real deal*, he thought.

"Cal, I'd like to know something," Eric announced.

Cal looked up without saying anything and gave Eric his full attention.

"After getting a letter like you got from Darlene, any other soldier around here who got one would have flipped out. They would've gone out and gotten ripping drunk, screamed and hollered at the moon, and made a total fool of himself. You didn't. Why?"

Cal chuckled. "My nana always told me that when we take on the job as one of Jesus' 'fishers of men,' we always have to be mindful of the bait we're using. If I went off cussin' and stormin', gettin' drunk and acting the fool and the like, the other soldiers would say, 'He's a phony. He's no better than us because he's acting just like we would.' I wouldn't be doing the job my Lord Jesus has given me to do. I would dishonor my Lord. That bait just wouldn't work, would it?"

"I have to admit if I got a letter like that from Julie, I wouldn't take too kindly to it either. I'm not sure what I'd do."

"I didn't take too kindly to it." Cal said. "I got blindsided by it. I just have to trust that God knows what He's doing. I had to work the thing out with my Lord. But make no mistake, it hurt. It hurt bad. I had planned to marry Darlene. I was going to finish my hitch in the army, go to school on the GI Bill, and then go into the ministry. The only part of that formula that's changed for now is the Darlene part. God may have more changes in the future; I don't know. I just have to trust Him. He didn't do this to me, but He allowed Satan to test my resolve and sincerity. He has another plan for who my partner will be. I might not even have a partner. I just have to trust Him."

Eric was amazed by his friend's faith. "I've told you before, Cal. I want the peace you have."

"When you're ready, let me know. Jesus is always ready to listen," Cal said.

"I think I'm just about ready," Eric said.

Cal chuckled again. "Eric, you're my good friend. But 'just about ready' won't cut it. I don't want you to be a 'lukewarm' believer—for your sake. In Revelation 3:16, Jesus said that He'd spew the lukewarm believer out of His mouth. Jesus and I want you to be a committed believer—a *follower* of Jesus. When you *know* you're ready, then we'll get down to it."

Eric looked across the room into Cal's eyes. "I want to be ready, Cal, but I'm scared."

"I get that. It's good to have a healthy fear of God. He's pure awesome. Proverbs 1 says that 'the fear of the LORD is the beginning of knowledge,' so you're beginning to be wise, my friend. But a fear of

Jesus is a misplaced fear, unless you're not one of His followers. Once you're His, you're His forever unless you turn your back on Him, like Judas did. Fortunately, though, just like Peter who denied Jesus three times just before the crucifixion, Jesus will forgive the truly repentant."

"You keep using words I've heard all my life in the church where I grew up, but nobody ever really explained them to me. Can you explain some of them?"

"Yes," Cal replied. "The problem you just expressed is widespread in the churches of today. It's called the apostate church. They teach people stories about Jesus and His life, but they don't teach people how to have a close, personal relationship with Him. Without a relationship with Jesus, they have no power. They're just marking time."

Just then, one of their roommates, "Big Smitty," six-three and hard as nails, came in. Most soldiers avoided Smith because he never shut up about his being from Independence, Missouri, where former President Truman was from. "You two Bible thumpers plotting to save the world?" Big Smitty asked with a sneer.

"Yes," answered Cal, adding, "and the blood of Jesus was shed for you, too, Smitty."

"I'm not going to sit here and listen to this," Smitty said and was out the door like a bow shot.

Eric's mouth dropped. "I've never seen Smitty run from anything."

"Have you ever heard someone say, 'there's power in the blood of Jesus,'?" Cal asked.

"Yes, but I never really knew what it meant."

"You just witnessed it," Cal said. "The dark always flees from the light, and the blood of Jesus will always win. I want you to think seriously about something, Eric. Jesus said in Matthew 16:24, 'If any man will come after me, let him deny himself, and take up his cross, and follow me.' Jesus wants serious followers, not the wishy-washy who run at the first sign of trouble. Matthew 16:25 continues, 'For whosoever will save his life shall lose it: and whosoever will lose his life for my sake shall find it.' Are you ready to make a commitment to following Jesus? You don't need to answer that right now. Like I said, I want you to think about it seriously."

Actually, Eric *had* been thinking about it seriously. He was positive that Cal was genuine. But he wondered if he had the guts to endure what he'd seen Cal subjected to. And he wondered quietly that if he weren't as genuine as Cal, would anyone ever know?

"And don't make the mistake," Cal continued, "of thinking that no one would ever know if you didn't really take your commitment to Jesus seriously. *Jesus* will know, and that's bad enough; but it will be obvious to other genuine believers as well."

Eric was beginning to think Cal could read his mind. "Cal, I think I'd like to be baptized. Maybe that would help me make the commitment. I was just sprinkled when I was a baby and didn't really know what was going on. I want to remember my baptism."

Cal smiled. "That's good, my friend. I'll talk with the chaplain about making that happen, but remember, baptism doesn't save you, only trust in what Jesus did for us on Calvary's cross saves us. Baptism is just a public expression of our faith in Him."

Cal had told the chaplain about the prayer journal he kept, and the chaplain asked if Cal would share it with him.

"Do you want me to go and get it now?" Cal asked. He was pleased the chaplain wanted to see it. His journal was a personal item, but he felt a kinship with his new boss.

"That would be good, Cal. You can go and get it while I make a phone call. I need to check with Rachel a little more often these days. She's going to have twins, you know."

Cal smiled. Yes, he knew the chaplain's wife was going to have twins. Yes, he knew that he was going to name the twin boys Joseph and Benjamin and that they were due any time now. And every time the chaplain told the story, his face beamed.

"Yes, sir, you've told me," Cal said.

Cal also knew, from Rachel's own lips, that she was going to have twin girls; and she was going to name them Josie and Bonnie. Cal also knew something neither Jacob nor Rachel knew and secretly wondered what they were going to do if she had one boy and one girl. And every time that thought crossed his mind, Cal chuckled. They were cute together. Even their bantering was chock-full of love for one another. Cal hurried off to his room to get his journal.

When he entered his room, he saw his roommate Big Smitty lying on his bunk, fully clothed including his boots, in the fetal position, face to the wall. *That's odd*, Cal thought. It was highly unusual to see Big Smitty moving at any speed short of full throttle. Cal never imagined Smith had a full-stop setting.

Cal got his journal from his locker and started to leave but stopped short and turned to Big Smitty. "You okay, Smitty?"

"Leave me alone, Buttinsky," he boomed.

"Okay, Smitty, I will for now. But if I can help you in some way . . . or if the chaplain can help . . . "

Smitty cut Cal off as he leaped from his bunk and got in Cal's face. "It's *your* God Who made my mom sick in the first place. And now *your* God is going to make her die. And I don't want my mom to die. I *love* her, and I *need* her." Tears were streaming down Smith's face, which had a pained and yet a softer look about it than Cal had ever seen before. Big Smitty was showing a human side new to Cal.

"Wow, Smitty, I'm so sorry," Cal said softly. "I'll tell the chaplain what's going on. Maybe he can help you like he helped me."

"What can *he* do to help me? All *you* lost was a girlfriend. Wah, wah. I'm going to lose my mom. Big difference."

"You're right, Smitty, it is a big difference. But the chaplain might be able to get you home to be with her before—"

"I'll believe that when I see it," Smitty said, cutting him off again and turning and throwing himself back onto his bunk, facing the wall, as before. As Cal left their room, Smith yelled over his shoulder, "You church types all talk peace and love; but when real trouble arrives, you scatter like cockroaches."

Cal left the barracks and hurried back to the chapel still feeling the sting of some of Smitty's words. He had to let the chaplain know what was going on with Smith. *Surely,* Cal thought, *the chaplain can do something!*

When he arrived back at the chapel, he found the chaplain had left but found a note on his own desk, which read, "I have to go to the airport to pick up my father-in-law. Back shortly." Cal felt a bit helpless. He wanted to do something to help Smith, but he was at a loss as to what form that help would take.

He sat down at his desk and dropped his head in his hands. "Think . . . think." Then, as if a bolt of lightning had hit him, he changed the chant to, *No! Pray! Pray!* He got back up from his desk and hurried into the chapel sanctuary and dropped to his knees on the kneeling pads. Cal was going to give Big Smitty's problem to the One Who solves problems best.

Cal was still on his knees praying when he heard the chaplain's voice. Cal got up from his knees and went in the direction of the voices.

"Oh, great! Cal, I want you to meet Rachel's father, Paul. He's here to meet his first grandchildren when they're born."

Cal extended his hand for a handshake feeling that he'd seen Paul before. "I feel like I know you from somewhere, sir." Cal said.

"Well, Cal, you may very well have seen me before. Where are you from?"

"I'm from East Saint Louis."

"On the Illinois side from Saint Louis, right?"

"Yes, sir."

"I'm from Missouri," Paul said. "I raised Rachel in Columbia, about dead center in the middle of the state. I was a pastor in an Assembly of God church there for many years."

"One of my roommates is from Missouri," Cal said. "Independence, Missouri. Do you know where that is?"

"Sure do. It's up just east of Kansas City. That's where former President Truman lives."

"That's what Big Smitty keeps telling us," Cal said as he turned to the chaplain, "and I wanted to talk to you about him, Chaplain. When I went back to the barracks to get my prayer journal, Big Smitty was curled up in his bunk with all his clothes and even his boots on. He was lying there in a ball. I think he'd been crying. I asked if he was okay, and he just jumped out of his bunk and yelled at me that it was my God's fault that his mother was dying and he couldn't get home to be with her. I offered to do something to help, but he accused Christians of being a bunch of cockroaches who scatter at the first sign of trouble."

"Has he ever mentioned anything about God, Cal?" the chaplain asked.

"No, all I ever heard him say is that he's an atheist."

"That's good," Paul said. "An atheist who blames God for adversity is something we can work with. He's unwittingly admitting that there just may be a God after all."

"Cal," the chaplain said, "can you take us to him? Maybe Paul can help him."

"Follow me," Cal said hurrying toward the door.

"Wait, Cal," the chaplain said, "We'll take my car. It'll be faster."

They arrived at the barracks, and Cal led the way to his room where Smitty was still lying on his bunk as before.

"Smitty," Cal said quietly when they arrived.

"I told you to leave me alone, Cal. Nobody can help me. Captain Blaylock said that Colonel Harkrider has forbidden me to go home on emergency leave."

"Smith," Paul spoke up. "I'm a United States senator from your home state of Missouri."

Smitty bolted up from his bunk and looked disbelievingly at Paul before recognizing him. "Yes, sir. I recognize you from photos I've seen."

"Has anyone bothered to explain to you the reason for denying your request for emergency leave?" Paul wanted to know.

"No. The colonel doesn't like me and doesn't believe my mom's sick. It doesn't matter that I have a notification from the Red Cross; they won't let me go."

"May I see the notification, please?" Paul asked.

Smitty got up and got the notice from his locker, handing it to the senator.

"May I take this notice, Smitty?" Paul asked again. "I'll bring it back after I've paid a visit to your Colonel Harkrider. Get your bags packed, young man. You're going home."

"Cal," the chaplain said, "stay here and help Smitty while Paul and I tend to some important business. We'll get together again later. Okay?"

Cal nodded, and the other two men left Smitty and Cal's room.

Smitty's wide eyes showed disbelief in what had just taken place. He looked at Cal with a puzzled look on his face. "How did you arrange that, Cal?"

"I didn't arrange it, Smitty. God did."

"Don't start with the God stuff again, Cal. You know I'm an atheist."

"Okay, let's say that's true. But I've heard you talk about your mom in the past, and you always say she's a religious woman. So, I'm guessing she's been praying for you for some time that you would, at some point, give your heart to Jesus. Don't you think that's true?"

"I guess so," Smitty admitted.

"So, let's go another step forward. Paul, the senator from Missouri you just met, is the father of the chaplain's wife, Rachel. You probably didn't know that, did you?"

"No, I didn't. I had no idea how you arranged that bombshell."

"I didn't arrange it," Cal said. "God did when Rachel prayed that her dad would be here for the birth of the twins. I heard her tell the chaplain she'd prayed for her dad to be here."

"Well, that explains the senator," Smitty said.

"And after I left our room earlier, I went back to the chapel and got on my knees to pray for God to reveal Himself to you and help you solve your problem."

"Well, you shouldn't have wasted your breath," Smitty almost snarled.

"And lastly, Mr. Atheist, you can't deny that when you were lying there on that bunk with your face buried in the wall, that you were begging the God you say doesn't exist to prove that He *does* exist by solving the problem you're facing—a problem which you cannot possibly solve for yourself. Whether you like it or not, you *were* praying. You probably thought 'no one will ever know,' but I know. You need not deny it. You see, when the senator arrived on this scene, he answered Rachel's prayer, my prayer, your prayer, and will ultimately answer your mother's prayers, too, when you surrender your heart to Jesus Christ. There are *never* any coincidences with God. These are all *Divine appointments.* God arranged all of this to reveal Himself to you, Smitty."

Smitty began to cry. Big Smitty, six foot three and tough as nails, was melting.

"When you're ready to make that commitment," Cal said quietly, "I'll be proud to help you." Cal extended his hand to shake Smitty's.

CHAPTER 11
THE TWINS ARRIVE

Later that afternoon, Cal and Eric were walking to chow. Eric was telling Cal about Horrible Harkrider being relieved of his command. "A three-star general with a U. S. senator and two M.P.s walked into old 'Horrible's' office and closed the door, and the M.P.s left with Harkrider in tow about twenty minutes later. The rumor is he was taken to the stockade awaiting court martial."

Cal shook his head. "I know he didn't treat his people right, but he must have been caught doing something pretty bad to be going up on charges bad enough for a court martial! God's Word says we always reap what we sow. The Living God knows where we are and what we're doing every moment of every day. We can't hide."

"Hey, guys, wait for me," Skip called from behind them. Cal and Eric stopped and waited for Skip to catch up. "Man, what a day," Skip said. "I guess you guys know about Horrible Harkrider, right? It couldn't happen to a nicer guy."

"That's pretty judgmental, Skip," Cal said. "Jesus told the Pharisees when they brought a woman caught in adultery that anyone who was without sin should cast the first stone when they wanted to stone her to death.[3] Are you without sin, Skip?"

---

3   John 8:7

"Well . . . no," Skip replied.

"God loves Colonel Harkrider as much as He loves you, Skip," Cal said.

"Well, what's not to love," Skip said, striking a silly pose.

"I know you intended that last remark as a rhetorical question, but I'm going to answer it, anyway. Let's start with cheating on your wife as something not to love," Cal answered.

"Everybody does it," Skip protested. "Besides, as I remember the story, Jesus forgave the woman caught in adultery. He'll forgive me, too."

"You're right, Skip," Cal continued. "Jesus forgave the woman, but do you remember what He told her after He said 'neither do I condemn thee'[4]?"

"No. Not really."

"He said, 'go, and sin no more.' First John 1:9 says, 'If we confess our sins, he [Jesus] is faithful and just to forgive us our sins and to cleanse us from all unrighteousness.' We must also repent. Repentance means what He told the woman: 'go, and sin no more.'"

"You're making too much of a big deal out of it, Cal. After I'm home, nobody will ever know I strayed. I'm a man and have needs, after all, I'm a scorpio."

"How would you feel if your wife said the same thing? Does she have needs, too?" Cal wondered aloud.

"That's different," Skip said, defending his blatant double standard.

"You're placing your trust in times and seasons rather than trusting the one who created those times and seasons," Cal said, "and when your misplaced trust in astrology fails you, and it will, you'll find Jesus in that void waiting for you with outstretched nail-scarred hands to accept you with his eternal love."

---

4   John 8:11

"I don't want to talk about this anymore," Skip said trying to duck the topic.

"That's not surprising," Eric finally contributed, "since you've caught yourself in your own web of deceit."

The three soldiers arrived at the chow hall, waited in line for their turn to have their trays loaded with their evening meal, and found an empty table. The atmosphere in the chow hall itself was far livelier than Cal had seen it in months. It was almost as giddy as the Munchkins singing "The Wicked Witch Is Dead" from the movie "The Wizard of Oz."

The trio ate their meals, mostly in silence, listening to the new good-natured attitudes of those around them. It was nice to see, Cal thought. The morgue-like silence from days past had disappeared.

"Corporal." Captain Blaylock's voice came from behind.

Cal turned and, recognizing his former captain, jumped to his feet and snapped to attention. "Yes, sir!"

"Stand easy, Corporal," he said. "The senator asked me to find you and bring you to the hospital. The chaplain's wife has gone into labor, and the chaplain wants you to be there."

Cal smiled, feeling very honored. "Yes, sir. Can I bring my roommate, Eric?"

"I see no reason why not," the captain said, then turned and addressed Skip. "You take their trays to the dishwashers." Skip nodded but did not look pleased about the assignment.

Cal and Eric followed the captain to his Jeep, and the three went speeding off to the hospital. Cal looked at the captain with a puzzled look. "With all due respect, sir, why did you get the detail to find me? I would have expected someone far more junior for the job."

Keeping his eyes on the road, the captain replied, "That senator took a huge monkey off my back when he got Horrible Harkrider canned today. Harkrider treated the enlisted men poorly, but his treatment of junior officers was horrendous. His nickname was given to him by his junior officers, not the enlisted types. I was more than happy for this assignment to find you. I'd do just about anything for a man like the senator. I'd sure vote for him if I didn't hail from Wyoming."

Eric said excitedly, "Where in Wyoming, captain? I'm from Cheyenne."

The captain smiled at Eric's revelation. "Casper's only about 180 miles away from Cheyenne. I sure miss trout fishing on the North Platte, don't you?"

"I sure do," Eric agreed. "I'm curious, captain. The rumor is that Colonel Harkrider was taken to the stockade. What in the world did he do that warranted a court martial?"

"I can't really discuss all the details, but he's been involved in criminal activity for some time—black market stuff. He's been in Army CID crosshairs for some time, and there were others they wanted to snag; but the events of today just brought everything to a head." The captain pulled his Jeep up to the hospital entrance.

"Here you are, boys. Give the good senator my regards." Captain Blaylock said in parting.

Cal thanked the captain for the lift, and he and Eric hurried to the waiting room where they found Paul and the chaplain sitting quietly waiting for news from the delivery room.

"Any word yet?" Cal wanted to know.

"Nothing yet," Paul and the chaplain said in unison, with the chaplain adding, "We wanted you here, Cal, to add the prayer of another believer to our prayer chain."

"I'm honored," Cal said. "I brought Eric along so we can add one more believer to the group!"

"That's great," Paul said. "The chaplain tells me you're wanting to be baptized, Eric. Is that right?"

Eric looked at Cal. *He did tell the chaplain*, he thought. "Yes, sir. I'd like that very much."

"That's wonderful, Eric. I had the privilege of baptizing the chaplain. Did you know that? I'm an ordained pastor."

"Wow, a man of many callings," Eric said.

"Yes, that happens when we become one of Jesus' fishers of men. We wind up wearing hats we didn't know would fit us. Maybe we can fit your baptism in while I'm here," Paul said.

"That would be nice, Paul," the chaplain said, "But we don't have a baptismal pool. I'm not sure where we can do it."

"Where there's a will and a willing lieutenant general wanting to make amends for a loose-cannon colonel, there's a way."

Just then a nurse in scrubs wearing a loosened surgical mask came into the waiting room and said, "Chaplain, you're the father of a baby girl. We'll know about the other baby in a few minutes." She left again.

Paul, Cal, and Eric smiled at a beaming chaplain. "Josie it is, I guess. Didn't get my Joseph. I guess Bonnie will be along in a few minutes."

Everyone was quiet for a couple of minutes until Eric broke the silence. "I always wondered what people who don't smoke give away instead of cigars when their babies are born."

Paul and the chaplain looked at one another for a couple of seconds and then laughed. "I hadn't given it a thought," the chaplain said. "Guess I'll have to buy some bubble gum."

The same nurse returned just then and announced, "You also have a son, Chaplain!"

Cal laughed. "I wondered what you'd do if you had one of each. You're not going to name him Bonnie, are you?"

"No, his name is Benjamin," the chaplain said from a glowing face. "Jacob and Rachel begat Josie and Benjamin."

Then the nurse said, "Your wife would like for you to come and meet your children, Chaplain."

CHAPTER 12
IN SPIRIT AND IN TRUTH

A week and a half after the twins were born was a Sunday. Cal asked Eric if he would come with him to the chapel to set up for Divine services. Eric agreed, and the two left the barracks and walked to the chapel, nearly a mile away.

"Cal," Eric said shortly after they set off, "I have a big question about prayer I need to ask. You call yourself a Pentecostal Christian. I'm not sure I know what that involves. Can you explain it to me?"

"Sure. But let's take a walk down your memory lane to help answer that question. What day does the Christian church call its birthday?"

"I don't know, Cal. Is it Pentecost?"

"Absolutely right. Pentecost is the day God the Holy Spirit baptized the apostles, giving them the ability to speak with unknown tongues. Their ability of tongues amazed those listening because the apostles were speaking in the native languages of their listeners, even though the apostles themselves didn't know what they were saying. Of course, there were other gifts given as well—prophecy, word of knowledge, and others—but the first apparent gift was tongues. Those who exercise the gifts of the Holy Spirit are Pentecostal Christians. It's a prayer tongue we use to talk to God as our best friend."

Eric thought about it for a moment, then said, "My church growing up said we don't do tongues anymore because of something it says in the Bible about tongues will cease."

"Yes, and every word of the Bible is God's Word and is true," Cal said. "Your church is referring to I Corinthians chapter thirteen verse eight, which says, 'Whether there be tongues, they shall cease.' That is a prophecy which refers to the end times. God gave us the gifts of the Spirit for those who will come to Jesus. As long as God the Holy Spirit has work to do on earth, He and the gifts will be active. When He has no more work to do, He will leave."

"I've never heard you talk in tongues, Cal. Do you?"

"Yes, I do. You've never heard me because it's a personal thing between me and Jesus. I pray in tongues when I'm happy. I pray in tongues when I'm sad. I pray in tongues whenever I just don't know what to say. Praying in tongues is not something to show off. We are not to flaunt our gifts. God humbles the proud and exalts the humble. God also blesses me with the gift of prophecy occasionally. For example, I knew the chaplain and his wife were going to have one boy and one girl, but I kept it to myself."

"Why didn't you tell anybody?" Eric asked. "I would have blabbed it all over."

"I didn't say anything because doing so would have served no useful purpose. I knew that God would reveal it in His good time. I just got the joy of chuckling to myself every time the chaplain and his wife would discuss whether they were having two boys or two girls. In the final analysis, they were both half-right and half-wrong. God even arranged to complete my joy by my being present when the chaplain and his wife discovered the truth."

"Well, that certainly explains why you were chuckling so loud and so long at the hospital. I wondered about that."

"Yup. That's why," Cal said. "Now, I want to get back to your understanding of tongues. First Corinthians thirteen verse eight says tongues will cease, which is what your church taught. But that is an example of man picking and choosing what parts of God's Word they feel comfortable teaching. It's not the full story."

"Yes, I get that, but I'm still not sure about how I feel about it."

"Okay, let's move from I Corinthians 13:8 to I Corinthians 14:39, where the apostle Paul, in the very next chapter says, 'Forbid not to speak with tongues.' Why would Paul say in one chapter no and in the very next chapter of the same book yes? Does that make sense? You will often hear Pentecostal churches referred to as Full Gospel. That's because Pentecostal churches don't pick and choose which verses of God's Word to believe and which verses to ignore. We believe and teach the *entire* Word of God."

"Well, I'm not sure if I want to go that far," Eric said. "I'm scared of it. And my wife, Julie, has never had any church experience in her life. I'm not sure she'd understand any sudden explosion of tongues."

"When I first prayed for the baptism of the Holy Spirit, I didn't exercise my prayer tongue either because, like you, I was a little apprehensive. Then the Holy Spirit led me down a path along which I clearly saw His hand in each step I took in obedience. It happened like this. About six weeks before I left for basic training, a man from church asked me to help him with some work he needed done around a rental house he owned. He said he'd pay me forty dollars when I was done. I was eager to do the work because I wanted to have some money in my pocket before I left for basic. It was hard work, and it took me several days to finish.

"I went to his house to get paid, and he wasn't there. And he wasn't in church for the next two Sundays. On the third Sunday, he was at church but said he didn't have any money with him and I should come by his house on the next Tuesday. I went to his house on Tuesday, and he wasn't there. I was starting to get steamed about it and complained to God in prayer. I told God that I'd worked hard to earn that money and reminded Him that His Word promised that He would bless the work of my hands. But that man from church dodged me, and I finally had to leave for basic without being paid for the work I'd done."

"That's terrible," Eric said. "Sounds like a deadbeat."

"On the surface, maybe, but that's not the end of the saga. Nana gave me twenty dollars to put in my pocket before I left so I wouldn't be completely broke, but I was plenty unhappy about doing a good job and then getting the stiff-arm. One of the greatest gifts of God the Holy Spirit is joy—unspeakable joy and peace. When I began hating the man from church for his treatment of me, I lost my joy and peace. I still read my Bible and spent time in prayer, but the joy and peace were not there. I prayed for the joy and peace to return, and God told me to forgive the debt. I said, 'You want me to do *what?* I worked hard for that money. He owes me.' God answered me by saying, 'For how much did I forgive you?' Then I realized that forty dollars didn't compare to what I'd been forgiven, and I cried and confessed my sin and told God that the debt was forgiven. What God said next totally unarmed me. He said, 'Tell *him* the debt is forgiven.'"

"Wow, Cal! What did you do then?"

"Well, I wanted my joy and peace back, so I had to figure out a way to let him know the debt was forgiven. I didn't know his address, even though I knew where he lived; so I wrote him a letter and sent it to Nana to pass on to him. Once I put that letter in the mail, my joy and peace returned."

"I have to say, Cal, I don't know if I would have done that. Forty bucks is too much to throw away."

"Wait, Eric. There's more. Two weeks after I mailed my letter, I got one back from him with forty dollars and a letter asking me to forgive him for trying to cheat me. I fell to my knees to praise my Lord; and for the first time in my life, I began praying in an unknown tongue. When we pray in tongues, we're always praying in His will because God the Holy Spirit is doing the praying. When I first received the baptism of the Holy Spirit, my prayer tongue sounded strange to me. Now, hardly a day goes by without me praying in tongues. But I pray in private."

"I certainly never knew it." Eric said. "You keep it to yourself well enough."

"Like I told you, it's personal. It's not something to show off."

As the pair arrived at the chapel, Eric noticed several U. S. Navy trucks parked next to the chapel, which also carried the SEABEE insignia on the doors.

"What in the world are navy trucks doing on an army base?" Eric wanted to know.

"The Navy SEABEES are the construction battalion arm of the navy. Before the Senator left to go back to Washington, he helped

General Short get a detachment of SEABEES to come and build a baptismal pool for the major. They start tomorrow morning."

"Major? What major?"

Cal chuckled. "Oh, didn't I tell you? The chaplain's been promoted to major."

CHAPTER 13
SMITTY RETURNS

The SEABEES had been making a terrible racket for almost a week constructing the baptismal pool. Cal knew they had to make *some* noise to make the pool happen, but he wished they could do it when he wasn't trying to study for the sergeant's exam scheduled for the next week.

The chaplain, with bright, shiny, new gold oak leaves proudly pinned to his collar, poked his head into Cal's office and said, "I have another appointment, Cal. I'll be back in about an hour."

Cal glanced at his watch. This was the fifth or sixth time in the last two weeks that the chaplain had left for "an appointment" at this exact time and had been gone for just over an hour each time.

"Gonna go check on Rachel and the little people?" Cal probed.

"Nope," was all the chaplain said, and he was off.

Cal thought it curious that the major was going someplace at the same time of day for an hour or so for multiple days without saying where he was going or with whom he was going to meet. Cal had to accept that it really wasn't any of his business and the chaplain probably had much larger fish to fry than Cal knew. But he still wondered.

He stuck his nose back into the sergeant's manual to read—and hopefully learn—something about rifle squad combat tactics, just in case he had to answer a question on the exam about that particular topic, though it wasn't likely he would ever need to use that knowledge. Alas, the noise coming from the construction crew made it difficult for Cal to concentrate. He got up and walked outside to watch the construction crew at work.

It was a nice July day in Bavaria, and Cal was glad to have a break. He walked around the chapel to where the baptismal pool was being built into the front of the chapel sanctuary. The job was taking a little longer than originally thought because the chapel structure had to be altered to accommodate the pool and associated plumbing so that pipes wouldn't freeze during Bavarian winters. Cal watched the hard-working SEABEES weave their magic in making the major's wish become a reality. They worked like a hive of bees and deserved their reputation, Cal thought. They were loud and boisterous, but not one man of the ten-man crew was a slacker.

A voice from behind him said, "Cal." He turned to find Big Smitty, looking very tired and haggard, his uniform looking like he'd slept in it for a week.

"Smitty! You're back," Cal said. "I'm glad to see you!"

"I just got back about an hour ago. I *really* need to talk to someone, and you said you'd help me before I left. I figure since you helped me so much before I left, you can probably help me again. I want to talk to you first, and then maybe we can get the chaplain involved later. Okay?"

"We can do that. Let's go get a cup of coffee. My office is no place to talk right now with all the construction noise."

The two set off for the base special services coffee shop. "What about your mom, Smitty?" Cal asked.

"She died, Cal. My dad's beside himself. He worked in the steel mill all his life, and Mom and Dad were savers. They never spent money on anything they thought frivolous. They grew up during the Great Depression and didn't trust banks much, so they stashed cash. I didn't understand why we couldn't have more because I knew they had money to spare. I had a little job at the Piggly Wiggly grocery store; but I didn't make much—not as much as I wanted to spend—so I would sneak into their stash and swipe money from them . . . a little bit here and a little bit there. Not much, really. I justified it because I knew they had a lot more where that came from. I said to myself, 'No one will ever know.'"

"But you know, right?" Cal said. "There isn't anything anyone ever does that God can't forgive, Smitty."

"Okay, Cal, but there's more. My poor dad used up most of the money he and mom stashed for her medical treatments and her burial. He would have had more if I hadn't been such a selfish brat. A little theft here and a little theft there adds up to a huge theft."

They arrived at the coffee shop and ordered two cups of coffee. "It's too crowded to talk here, Smitty," said Cal. "Let's take this conversation on the road, so we can have some privacy."

Smitty nodded and the two walked away from the shop. The direction wasn't important to them, only the privacy.

"It's obvious to me, Smitty, that you have much more to unload. People talk about folks carrying baggage. Looks to me you're carrying cargo." Cal meant it as a joke, but Smitty didn't appear to be amused. He was hurting.

"I want my parents to forgive my selfishness, Cal," Smitty said with pain plainly spread across his face. "But now I can never have my mom's forgiveness because she's gone." Smitty began to cry. "And I have no idea how to ask my dad for his forgiveness."

Cal said nothing. The two walked without talking for several minutes with Smitty sobbing softly.

"Aren't you going to say anything, Cal? Are you being judgmental in your silence? If you are, I don't need it."

"I'm not judging you, Smitty. Far from it. I'm letting you get your pain and remorse out. When those are history, we can go to work on it."

"Well, then, at least tell me what you're thinking. I need to know."

"First, you're not telling me anything I haven't felt or done myself. My nana raised me. A couple of years ago, I wanted to buy something nice for my girlfriend's birthday, but I didn't have quite enough money for it. I knew where nana kept her 'cash stash,' as she called it, and 'borrowed' some. Turns out, she knew *exactly* how much money was there and asked me about the missing money. I was crushed and horribly embarrassed. I professed to be a Christian and was caught as a thief. Nana and God forgave me."

"How much did you take?" Smitty wanted to know.

"The amount isn't important. Whether you steal one penny or a million dollars, the sin is the same in God's eyes."

"That doesn't sound right. There's a big difference between a penny and a million bucks. How can it be the same in God's eyes?"

"Because the amount isn't the sin. The act is the sin," Cal replied.

Smitty was quiet for a few minutes as they walked further. He took a sip of coffee. "Okay, Cal. I have another question for you. What about homosexuality?"

Cal tried to act as though he wasn't completely blindsided by Smitty's question, even though he was. "What about it?"

"Well, I've heard some people say that God hates it," Smitty said. "My mom said He does."

"Let me ask you this, Smitty. What does God say about adultery?"

"Well, that's breaking one of the Ten Commandments isn't it?"

"That's right," Cal said. "Both adultery and homosexuality are sexual sins, and God condemns sexual sin in general. And although He hates the act of the sin, He loves the sinner. My nana says no sin is worse than any other sin, and God's Word bears that to be true. God sees them all the same. Coveting a penny is the same as murder to Him. God sees all disobedience the same. Jesus told us that failure in one point of the law is failure of all of it. But Jesus took all that failure upon Himself when His blood was shed, He died and was resurrected. Do you know about the woman who was taken in the act of sin during the Feast of Tabernacles and was brought before Jesus by the Pharisees to accuse her?"

"I sort of remember a story like that from when I was a kid in Sunday School."

"The story is in John chapter eight. The woman was caught in the very act of adultery. The Pharisees wanted her stoned in accordance with the Law of Moses. The Pharisees were actually testing Jesus. The fact that the woman was guilty was irrelevant to them. They just wanted to put Jesus on the spot. They didn't care about her; they only cared about their own power and self-righteousness. But Jesus forgave her and told her, 'Go, and sin no more.' Whatever wrongs you find yourself struggling with, Jesus is willing and able to forgive and remove. All you have to do is ask for His forgiveness and then be obedient and, 'Go, and sin no more.' The shed blood of Jesus cleanses us from all unrighteousness and replaces our sin with His righteousness. We become sin-free. It sounds like you are in need of that kind of forgiveness. Am I right?"

"I am, Cal. The last time you told me that the blood of Jesus was shed for me, I ran. It was like my ears and heart were on fire, and it scared me."

"I know your mom was praying for you to come to this point in your life when you would have to make a decision for Jesus. She wanted you to join her in eternity. She wanted this for you, but she knew that you had to make the decision for yourself. Making a reservation for entrance to Heaven is yours alone to do."

Smitty was nodding his head. "I know. Mom aways told me that I had to do it for myself."

The two had walked far enough to see the stockade ahead of them. Cal was surprised to see the chaplain just walking out.

"It's time we go back to the chapel, Smitty. Maybe we can visit with the chaplain. You probably don't know, but he was promoted to major while you were gone."

Chaplain Jacob, as his fledgling flock had begun to call him, stepped from the stockade entrance and walked slowly to his car. Today's meeting with the prisoner had been far more stressful than before. *This guy is like Jekyll and Hyde,* he thought. *One day, he's open and honest; the next time, he's closed and belligerent.* This day had been the latter multiplied by a factor of ten, which made him feel like he'd lost all the ground he thought he'd gained.

He got in his car and said to himself, "I've just got to keep praying for him. There has to be some good in there somewhere." He bowed his head and lifted the prisoner to the Lord.

Jacob finished his prayer, started the car's engine, and backed out of his parking spot, intending to return to the chapel and check on the progress of his pet project. Along the way, he thought he saw Cal and another soldier walking on the sidewalk headed in the direction of the chapel. He pulled to a stop beside them.

"Cal, want a ride?" Then he recognized the soldier walking with Cal. "Smitty! You're back."

"Yes, sir," Smitty replied.

"Well, get in, fellas, and we'll all go back together."

"This is great, Chaplain. Smitty says he wants to speak with you, anyway," Cal said as both he and Smitty got into the back seat of the car.

The chaplain looked at Smitty and said, "Mercy, Smitty! You and your uniform look like you just came out of two weeks in combat. Are you okay?"

"I'm doing better since I've spoken with Cal; but I've been traveling for several days, and lengthy travel isn't easy on either the man or the uniform he's wearing."

"Yes, I'd forgotten how unforgiving lengthy travel can be on us," the chaplain said as he put the car in gear and resumed the trip. "What did you want to talk with me about? Is it about your family problem?"

"No, sir," Smitty said softly. "My mom died. What I want to say, I want to say behind closed doors . . . please."

"Sure, Smitty. I understand."

The three were silent for several minutes until the chaplain spoke. "Hey, Cal. Isn't that your friend Eric running there on the sidewalk?"

"Looks like him," Cal said.

The chaplain pulled the car up beside the runner and said, "Eric, where are you headed? Want a ride?"

The heavy-breathing Eric stopped and said, "I was just headed to see you, and I sure could use a ride. Your stopping takes care of both." Eric hopped in the front seat and struggled to catch his breath. He looked in the back seat and was surprised to see Smitty. "Smitty! You're back! I didn't think we'd ever see you again."

"It's me," Smitty replied. "I just got back this morning."

"I don't mean to be rude, but you look terrible," Eric said.

"I've been told," was all Smitty had to say about it.

"I'll be happy to talk with you, Eric," the chaplain said, "but Smitty's tossed his hat in the ring first. You can be first after him, okay?"

"Sure, that's all right, but let me give you and Cal a preview. I got a letter from my wife, Julie, today, and she and my little boy are coming here to be with me. I need to find someplace for her to live, and I don't know if I can qualify to get on-base housing or not. I just have so many questions needing answers, I thought you could help me with all of this."

Cal jumped in. "Wow, Eric! That's great!"

"We'll certainly do what we can," Chaplain Jacob replied, smiling. He was silently thanking and praising Jesus for this wonderful ministry assignment. It was taking on dimensions of which he'd never dreamed—mountain top to valley and back again. *El Shaddai is good all the time*, he thought, *and all the time El Shaddai is good.*

They arrived at the chapel; and as the occupants unloaded themselves, it appeared as though they were coming out of a clown car.

"Smitty," the chaplain said, "come into my office, and, Eric, you can have a chair until Smitty and I are finished, okay?"

Both men nodded their assent as Smitty followed the major into his office. He closed the door behind Smitty and pointed to a chair. "Have a seat, Smitty." The major sat on the same side of his desk as Smith. "Now, what's on your mind?"

"Well, sir, I have to know that what I say here will remain between us," Smitty began.

"I can assure you, Smith, whatever we discuss will go no further than these four walls."

"That's good. I have some things I have to unload before I go crazy, and I have to know it's safe to shed myself of this weight."

The chaplain saw tears forming in the corners of Smitty's eyes. "Go ahead, Smith. Pour your heart out. It's safe here."

Smith put his face in his hands and started sobbing. He was trying to talk through his sobs; but the chaplain couldn't make out his words, so he just let Smitty sob until he was sobbed out.

"I heard you trying to talk to me just now," the chaplain said, "but I couldn't make out what it was you were trying to tell me."

Smitty straightened up and cleared his throat. He told the chaplain about his guilt over stealing from his parents for so long. "I thought no one would ever know," he concluded, "but I know."

Chaplain Jacob said a silent prayer for wisdom before addressing the broken soldier in front of him: "Smitty, when Jesus was nailed to that Roman cross so long ago, every sin of you and me and everyone else who ever lived was nailed to that cross with Him. And when He died and was resurrected, every one of those sins were forgiven. Even sins neither one of us have committed yet were forgiven. All we have to do is confess and repent. Do you want to be forgiven, Smitty?"

"Yes," he replied. "I want this pain to go away. I want to see my mom again. I want Jesus in my life, Chaplain. I want . . . I *need* His love and forgiveness."

CHAPTER 14
GULP!

Cal was sitting at his office desk trying to read Chaplain Jacob's sermon for the coming Sunday. "Trying" was the operative word here. He was having trouble focusing on the sermon as his mind kept wandering off into the land of "what if"? He'd taken the sergeant's exam the week before and thought he should know the results by now. What if he hadn't passed the exam? Although he was elated for Chaplain Jacob's success in growing the kingdom of God from three to almost fifteen in regular attendance on Sunday, he was also concerned about his own success.

"Come on, Cal," he said aloud to himself. "Keep your head on the task at hand. You'll know when God wants you to know."

Just then, he heard the front door of the chapel slam. He jumped to his feet to investigate as Chaplain Jacob swept into his office. He did not look happy, which was a new image for Cal's mind to process.

"Stand at attention, soldier!" the chaplain ordered.

Cal complied, snapping to attention, eyes focused on an imaginary object on the horizon, thumbs pressed into the sides of his trousers, back straight as a ramrod, and issuing a crisp, "Yes, sir."

His mind was unable to comprehend what was happening. Was this real?

"So, soldier, you think you're ready to put on sergeant's stripes, do you? What makes you think you're qualified? Don't you think you should be able to pass a test first? Didn't I give you the manual to study so you *could* pass that exam? What do you have to say for yourself, Sergeant?"

Cal didn't know what to say. His mind was blank. *Wait.* "What did you call me, sir?"

Chaplain Jacob smiled broadly. "I said, what do you have to say for yourself, Sergeant?"

"Sergeant?" Cal whispered with his church voice.

"Congratulations, Sergeant Cal. I've known about your promotion for several days, but I wanted to tell you on the actual day of your promotion. Your sergeant's pay starts as of today." Chaplain Jacob held out his hand as if to shake Cal's hand. As Cal put his hand out to shake the chaplain's, Jacob turned his hand over to reveal sergeant stripes. "Here, get these sewn on your uniform. I want you to be in uniform with the proper rank insignia."

"Thank you, sir, but with all due respect, Chaplain, you know how I was fretting over this whole sergeant thing. This was kind of ornery of you. It's a side of you I've never seen before."

"Jehovah Jireh used the ornery streak He gave me to make the day of your promotion to sergeant a memorable one. How did we do?"

Cal chuckled. "I'm not likely to forget this any time soon!"

The chaplain winked and said, "Now you can let Jehovah Shalom take over."

Then Cal said again, softly, "Sergeant!"

———————— .✦. ——

Chaplain Jacob arrived at the stockade five minutes before he was scheduled to meet with the prisoner—again. *What is this,* he thought to himself, *nine times this guy has called to meet with me?* For what purpose, Jacob could only guess, because his behavior was all over the map. He bowed his head and breathed a quick prayer before going inside.

"Adonai, I have no idea why You keep putting me together with this man, but You do. I ask that Your will be done in this matter, in Your way and in Your time, and that You will be glorified in the outcome. I love You, Lord, and I trust Your outcome." He got out of his car and went inside and jumped through all the hoops for entry—again.

Upon entering the visitor's room, Jacob noticed that Curtis was not on the other side of the wire mesh divider. "I thought I was going to visit with Curtis," he said.

"Well, Chaplain, I asked to see you instead. Curtis just wanted to try to pull you through the knothole backwards, anyway. He bragged about how he twisted things you said and tried to make you look foolish. He even threw the Bible you gave him across the cellblock. I have that Bible now. I've been reading it. But you need not call me Colonel Harkrider any longer. Just call me Ben."

"All right, Ben. I have to admit I'm surprised you want to see me, but do you have any questions you want to ask me?"

"Yes, but I want you to know a little bit about me first. I grew up in a little town in Texas called Bedford. That's between Dallas and Fort Worth. We lived on a street named Brown Trail. I always thought Brown Trail sounded very Texan."

The chaplain nodded in agreement. "It does indeed sound like it should be a Texas street."

"My dad was a civilian maintenance man at Naval Air Station Dallas," Ben continued. "My folks were regular church-goers at a little Baptist church in Bedford, not far from our house. My mom was always pestering me to get baptized, but I wasn't really interested in church things. I had what I thought were bigger plans and saw church as a roadblock to what I wanted for my life. So, I never went through with it. I joined the army toward the end of World War II and decided to stay in. I fought in Korea and got involved in some things there that have ultimately landed me here. At first, I thought, 'No one will ever know.' What I discovered over time, though, is that the more we tell ourselves that no one will ever know, the sloppier we get.

"Before long, a guy gets nabbed because he gets sloppy. My dad was a quiet guy, who spoke great wisdom, which I ignored. He told me that God is patient but always gives us enough rope to hang ourselves. One of my dad's favorite Bible quotations was 'Your sin will find you out.'[5] When he said that, I always thought, 'Yeah sure, but not if you're smart.' Long story short, I'm facing at least ten years at Fort Leavenworth—maybe longer . . . because I *wasn't* smart."

"Okay," Jacob said, "what is it that you want me to help you with?"

"I was reading in the Bible you gave Curtis about the crucifixion of Christ, and I was struck by the similarities between the criminals crucified on either side of Jesus and Curtis and me." Ben paused for several seconds, hoping to see some recognition of his point in the face of the chaplain.

5   Numbers 32:23

"Okay, Ben, I think I'm following you," Jacob said, nodding slowly.

"Well, Curtis keeps mocking you like one of the criminals mocked Jesus; but the other criminal who was not as hateful to the Jesus was told by the Lord, 'This day shalt thou be with me in paradise.'[6] We don't know anything else about that criminal, yet Jesus promised him Heaven."

"Right," Jacob said. "Go on."

"Well, it got me to thinking about that criminal entering Heaven right off that cross, with no time to even show he had changed. I think if I had seen him coming in, I would have asked him, 'How did you get in here?' Do you know what I think that criminal would have said?"

Jacob smiled and said, "No, but I'm certainly interested in hearing what you think."

"I think he answered, 'Because the Man on the middle cross invited me.'"

"Ben, that may be one of the most profound things I've ever heard about the crucifixion. It certainly puts that event into a perspective I'd not heard or seen before."

Ben smiled that his thoughts were appreciated. "I've been invited all of my life—mostly by my mom and dad, but there have been a few other invites along the way as well. I think it's high time I accepted the invitation."

"Good decision, Ben. How do you see us proceeding in your present circumstances?"

"I was hoping you'd have some of those answers. I very much want to be baptized like my folks wanted, and I hear you're having a baptismal pool built. Is that right?"

---

6 Luke 23:43

"Yes, it's actually complete. We can't use it for two more weeks, though, because the SEABEES who built it tell me it has to cure— whatever that means." Jacob said. "I guess that gives us at least two weeks to see what we can get done on your behalf. I'll make some calls."

"Well, Chaplain," Ben said with a huge smile, "from what I hear, your calls generally produce results. I'm counting on you."

Jacob left the stockade and returned to his car. He got in and, before he started the engine, bowed his head in thanks. "Elohim, the Great I Am, thank You for showing me why I've been visiting here and for showing me, once again, that Your word never returns void."

CHAPTER 15
THE APARTMENT

E ric hurried into the chapel and immediately heard Chaplain Jacob
speaking with someone. He looked in Cal's office. Cal had placed
his index finger pointing up across his lips as if to tell Eric to proceed
quietly, which Eric did.

"Yes, General, I'm aware it poses a security risk," the chaplain said,
then fell silent for a few seconds, listening. "With all due respect,
General, that's exactly why we have military police—to address those
security issues."

Then he was silent again.

"No, General, I have no intention of involving the senator. I'm
sure we can come to some kind of arrangement on this issue. Our job
is addressing the spiritual needs of all soldiers, even prisoners."

Silence again.

"All I'm asking is that you give it some thought. He asked me to
check into it, and that's what I'm doing. Just let me know. I'm going to
be doing baptisms in the baptismal pool you got built for us in about
two weeks."

Silence.

"Yes, sir, we'll speak again soon."

"Cal," Chaplain Jacob called.

"Yes, sir," Cal replied jumping up from behind his desk to go to the chaplain's office to see what he wanted.

"One of the things the general wanted was to tell me that we will be losing our receptionist next month because she'll be going back to school. We'll have to find a replacement for her. Our little flock is growing, and we'll need someone with a few more skills than the girl we presently have. I have a hunch that some of the people who've begun attending church on Sunday are just here out of curiosity. We get things done, and maybe they think they might get in on some of the goodies. Do you know of anyone who might fill in for our girl?"

No, sir, I don't, but I'll keep my ear to the ground. You asked for Eric. He's here."

"Good. Eric, come in. You, too, Cal."

The two friends entered Chaplain Jacob's office, and he gestured to them to sit in the two chairs in front of his desk. "Eric, it's taken a bit of doing, but I've been able to pin down a small apartment not far off post for you and your wife to take. It's fully furnished, and the price is reasonable. There are two small bedrooms, plus another small room, probably intended to be a pantry, that could be used for the baby's room. That would give you and your wife a private bedroom, and the other bedroom can be occupied by your wife's friend. I've put a small deposit down on it for you. I really think it would serve your purposes well. Do you want to see it?"

"I absolutely do, Chaplain," Eric said excitedly. "They're going to be here next week. I know it would ease Julie's mind, not to mention her mother's mind, to know that we have a permanent place to lay our heads. Thank you for your help."

"Well, fellas, let's jump in the car and go look!"

Cathy stacked the last box from Julie's old apartment. "That's the box we've been looking for," Cathy said. "The last one." Julie's mom had cleared out a corner of her basement for Julie's things to be stored while she was away.

"How about some lunch, girls?" Barb called down her basement stairs.

"Great!" both girls exclaimed at the same time and hurried toward the stairs.

Barb had already set the table and had plated BLT sandwiches on three plates. "These tomatoes are from my next-door neighbor's garden. She just picked them this morning."

"Oh, yummy! Fresh, home-grown tomatoes are the best," Cathy said.

The three women all sat down. Cath and Jules each reached out to hold the other's hand, and both girls reached their other hands toward Barb. "Mom, please join us in our giving thanks for the meal."

Barb looked from Julie to Cathy and back again, not knowing exactly what to do, she just took their hands and bowed her head.

Cathy took the lead. "Holy, holy, holy, Lord. Almighty Father. The Great I AM. Thank You for providing for all our needs. Thank You for keeping all of Your promises. Thank You for Your mercy and grace. We ask that You bless the meal set before us to the nourishment of our bodies, and we ask that You bless our bodies to Your eternal glory. We ask that You bless the loving hands that prepared the meal. We pray in the precious name of our Lord and Savior, Jesus Christ. Amen."

Julie also said, "Amen."

Barb was silent, looking somewhat uncomfortable, maybe even embarrassed.

Cathy broke the silence. "Now that your things are safe and sound, I can tell you that I've found someone to take my apartment while I'm gone so I don't even need to move anything."

"That's great, Cath!" Julie exclaimed. "Who?"

"She's a girl I work with at the air force base. She's been living with her folks and wants a place on her own. She'll just take over my lease without even paying a deposit. Since I rented a furnished apartment in the first place, I just have clothes and some kitchen items. I'll leave the clothes I'm not taking to Germany at my folks' house and leave some of the kitchen items for Sue. Poof—no more problem."

"Air force base?" Barb asked. "I thought you were a shipping clerk."

"Well, I'm actually a receiving clerk, but I work at Warren Air Force Base. I have a government job; and once you have a background with the government, you can get another government job somewhere else as long as you have good management performance reviews, which I do. Who knows? I might want to get a job on base in Germany. I might like Germany and decide to stay there permanently."

"I want to change the subject, girls," Barb said. "While I was making the arrangements for your passports and checking on the need for travel visas, I decided that I would get one for myself as well. I'm going on this adventure with you. I've never been anywhere, and I've never actually done anything adventurous. I decided it was time I do. I certainly have enough money to do anything I want to do . . . so . . . I'm going along, too!"

Julie squealed with delight. "Oh, Mom! That's great. I always wanted to do something like this with you."

"One thing, though, girls," Barb said. "I know you're both religious. But no preaching to me. Okay?"

Cathy smiled at Barb and said, "There will be times during our trip when you will see things happen which defy explanation. You will ask questions about how it happened that way. Do you not want your questions answered?"

"I just can't imagine that happening," Barb replied without answering Cathy's question.

"That's because you don't know our Lord," Cathy said as the doorbell rang.

Barb went to the door and returned with an envelope. "It's a telegram. It must be bad news."

"Telegrams aren't always bad news," Cathy said.

"Who's it for, Mom?" Julie asked.

"It's for you."

"Who's it from, Mom?

"Eric."

Julie exchanged a knowing glance with Cathy. "Well, open it and read it, Mom!"

Barb looked at the envelope in her hand as if it were a venomous snake. She opened it and read it. She smiled.

"Read it, Mom."

Barb looked at Julie, then Cathy, and read, "Furnished apartment secured. All is ready here. Come."

CHAPTER 16
THE TRIP

The taxi arrived at 6:25 a.m. for the trip to the airport. They had all slept at Barb's house. Eric didn't want to get up and had to be coaxed awake with a piece of banana. There wasn't enough room in the trunk of the taxi for all the luggage, so two pieces had to be conveyed inside the cab, which left less room for people. Fortunately, the trip to the airport was a short one.

"Okay, girls," Barb said as their taxi ride began, "today is going to be a long day. Our first trip will be from here to Kansas City, where we'll change planes and then go on to Idlewild Airport in New York City. We're going to spend the night in New York to rest up before we go on to Europe. Since our flight to Europe will board at 7:00 p.m. tomorrow night, we'll be able to get plenty of rest and see some of the sights in New York tomorrow—maybe the Statue of Liberty."

"Oh, Mom! I've always wanted to see that. What about the Empire State Building? Can we see it, too?"

"What we get to see tomorrow depends on how late of a start we get in the morning," Barb replied.

They arrived at the airport a few minutes later. Little Eric was unable to keep his eyes open, and Julie had to carry him. Barb arranged for a skycap to carry all the luggage to the ticket counter, where their baggage was taken and they checked in for the flight. She tipped the skycap extravagantly, as was her custom. They walked the short distance to the gate and sat quietly, awaiting the boarding of their flight.

Little Eric was still sleeping with his head on Julie's shoulder when the flight was called to board. The little boy barely stirred as Julie put him in the outboard seat and strapped him in. The stewardess brought Julie a couple of pillows for the lad without even being asked. Julie took the aisle seat next to little Eric, and Barb and Cathy took the two seats across the aisle. Their plane took off about five minutes late, and Eric slept through the whole thing. Julie was elated.

"I was able to get four seats together for this flight only," Barb told the girls. "For the Kansas City to New York and New York to Paris flights, you girls and Eric will be sitting together; but I had to get my seat in first class."

"Hmmm," Julie mused. *Had to? Sounds like typical Mom,* she thought.

Little Eric woke up about three-fourths of the way to Kansas City. Julie had the foresight to put part of a banana and some breakfast O's in a wax-paper bag for him to munch on, as much to keep him quiet as to satisfy his hunger. It worked.

They landed in Kansas City and Julie watched out her window as the ground crew pushed a ramp up to the side of their plane for the passengers to unload. She also saw out her window a much larger, majestic-looking plane painted all white with two red stripes painted down its side and having three tails. She'd never seen such a beautiful plane before. She didn't even know there was one like that.

"Look, Cath, at that beautiful plane."

"I can't see it."

"Come over here and look out my window," Julie urged.

Cathy got up and went across the aisle to peer out Julie's window. "Wow. What is that? I've never seen an airplane like that before. It's huge . . . and three tails!"

The four exited the plane and went down the ramp to the ground. Julie looked toward the beautiful plane with three tails, and it looked even bigger and more beautiful than it had before. "Wow," she said breathlessly in appreciation to the plane's splendor.

They entered the terminal and asked the airline official at the arrival desk where the gate could be found for the flight to New York. The airline official told them, and off they went. Along the way, Barb told the girls, "Don't worry about our luggage. It will automatically be transferred to our plane to New York." Under her breath, she said, "I hope."

When they arrived at the proper gate and got checked in, Cathy pointed out the beautiful plane with three tails outside the gate window. The three tails looked like three upright boat rudders reaching into the sky. "Look, Julie," she said pointing to the window.

"Come on, Cath," Julie said and headed toward the window next to a stately man in a khaki suit, white shirt and no tie, reading a newspaper.

"Wow, Julie! That is an impressive-looking plane. I wonder what it is?"

The man sitting there put down his newspaper and told them, "It's called a Lockheed Constellation. Its nickname is 'Connie.' It's a beauty, don't you agree?"

"Yes," both girls said dreamily.

"We're going to New York, sir." Julie said. "Is that the plane that's going to take us there?"

"Yes, it is. I'm going there myself," he said, extending the hand of friendship to them to shake. "My name's Paul."

Julie put her hand out to shake Paul's. "I'm Julie, and this is my friend, Cathy. My mom and son, over there, are going with Cathy and me to Germany so my husband and I can be together."

"Good for you, Julie. My daughter, her husband, and my two grandchildren are in Germany, too. I'm on my way to see them."

"Wow," Julie said. "What a coincidence."

Paul smiled. "As a Christian, I don't believe in coincidences—only Divine appointments. I believe Jesus arranges for us to meet people for His purposes and glory."

"Cathy and I are Christians, too, but I never thought about how God might arrange for us to meet people. It makes sense, though."

"Julie's a fairly new Christian, Paul," Cathy said. "She's just learning how wonderfully awesome our Lord is."

Just then, the announcement was made for all first-class passengers to board. "That's me," Paul said picking up his things.

"It was nice to meet you, Paul," Cathy said. "I hope we can visit more later."

Paul waved. "We probably will. It's a long way to Germany."

As he walked toward the gate, Paul prayed, "Lord, I know You have a reason for this 'chance' meeting. You never have accidental events in the lives of Your saints. You always have purpose in what You do. If your purpose is just that I pray for the safety of the girls I just met, so be it. I plead the blood of Jesus on their trip and safety. If Your purpose is more than that, so be it. You will present your will as it unfolds. And as always, I pray that Your perfect will be done. Amen."

Paul presented his ticket to the gate agent and was wished a nice flight. He exited the terminal, climbed the boarding steps, and was greeted by the stewardess.

"Welcome aboard, Senator. It's nice to see you again. Your seat is the window seat in the third row back to your right."

Paul nodded. "Thank you."

After taking his seat, Paul reopened the *Kansas City Star* newspaper he'd been reading in the terminal and returned to an article about a man who had just announced his bid to run against him in the next U. S. Senate race in Missouri. As other first-class passengers boarded and took their seats, Paul continued to read his paper and paid little attention to the hubbub around him.

A woman stopped at the seat next to Paul and placed her carry-on items in the overhead bin above her seat. She sat down and, looking at Paul, said, "Aren't you the man I saw talking with my daughter and her friend?"

Paul looked up from his paper. "If you're Julie's mom, then yes, I am."

"Yes, I'm Julie's mom. My name is Barb," she said, extending her hand to shake his.

He took her hand. "I'm Paul. I'm happy to meet you, Barb."

"Julie said you're on your way to Germany, too."

"Yes, I'm going to visit my daughter and her family. Her husband is in the army in Stuttgart."

"Now, isn't that a coincidence! Julie's husband is in the army in Stuttgart, too. Maybe Eric and your son-in-law know one another."

Paul nodded, saying nothing about his view on coincidence.

"What does your son-in-law do in the army?" Barb wanted to know.

"He's a major. He's actually the command chaplain."

At Paul's announcement, Barb ceased talking for a while as other passengers boarded the "Connie." Paul returned to his newspaper, finished the article he'd been reading, folded the newspaper, and put it in the seat-back pouch in front of him. He reclined his seat, closed his eyes, and tried to put the article out of his mind for a few minutes.

Where do journalists get this stuff? he wondered.

The next thing Paul knew he was startled awake by the sound of the plane engines roaring to life. Paul had apparently to drifted into a shallow sleep.

The stewardess came by and said, "Senator, will you please put your seat in its upright position in preparation for take-off?"

"Certainly," he said as he moved his seat back to the forward position.

"Senator," Barb asked, looking at Paul. "You're a senator?"

"Yes, Barb. I'm a U. S. senator from the state of Missouri."

"Oh my," she said extending her hand again to shake his. "It is *indeed* an honor to meet you!"

"The honor is mine," Paul replied. "You and people like you are my boss. I serve the people."

"That's refreshing. Most of the politicians I hear talking on TV or radio and even in newspapers are pretty much out for themselves, and phooey on the little guy."

"Sadly, Barb, there are politicians who behave badly. I try not to be one of those because it would reflect poorly on my King, Jesus Christ."

"Why do you Christians always have to bring *Him* into every conversation? My daughter and her friend Cathy do it, too. It makes me very uncomfortable."

"To answer your question directly, Barb, we talk about Him because we know and love Him intimately. There isn't anything or anyone we can talk about more interesting than Him."

"I'm sorry, Paul. I cannot believe in a God who allows the kind of cruelty and torment He allowed during World War II. Millions of poor Jewish people were murdered. People all over Europe lost homes and businesses and even their very lives. And we lost so many of our brave military service men and women. The chaos and loss of life just makes me want to cry."

"I, too, mourn the losses experienced during that war. It might interest you to know that God Himself also mourns those lost. You and many other people who don't know Him blame Him for the actions of men. He is no more responsible for the bad behavior of men during that war than I'm responsible for the bad behavior of other politicians."

"Well, I blame Him for not stopping those bad men," Barb responded. "He could've stopped them from doing those awful things."

"Okay," Paul said, "let's look at the bad actions of others from a different perspective. Let's look at it from the perspective of God's gift of free will to all mankind. You have the gift. I have the gift. Julie and Cathy have the gift. We can all do pretty much whatever comes into our heads. But Adolf Hitler, Mussolini, the Japanese emperor and their followers also had the same free gift. The awful things they chose to do make the rest of us sick, but they did as they chose. God cannot go back on His word. If He did, we couldn't trust Him. If He took away their free will, He would also have to take away our free will. We have to trust that He will ultimately bring good from the evil around us."

They were both quiet for several minutes until Paul added, "Just think about what I've said for a while."

Barb started to open her mouth to say something else, then apparently thought better of it. "Okay. I'll think about it."

Paul closed his eyes again. He knew from the way she answered his last statement so abruptly that the gears of her mind were searching for yet another excuse for her disbelief. He knew it would just be a matter of time before she shot at him with something else. *Lord,* Paul prayed silently, *is this the reason for today's Divine appointment?* He didn't have to wait long.

"I've heard of something called evolution," Barb said. "How what we see around us and the stars and planets just happened. I think they call it the 'Big Bang.' The people who talk about it say that God doesn't exist. What do you think about the 'Big Bang'?"

Paul thought for a minute before opening his eyes. "If I gave you a box with ten puzzle pieces in it and told you to shake the box until the puzzle put itself together, how long do you think it would take you to accomplish the task?"

"That's impossible to know. I'm not even sure it's possible to do."

"Well, Barb, if you're not sure if it's possible to put together only ten small puzzle pieces by chance, what do you think is the likelihood of putting together trillions and trillions and trillions of other random pieces in some semblance of order by chance? Don't you think it would take an intelligent Designer to piece together the wonders of God's creation? To me, it takes more faith to believe it's all an accident than to believe in an awesome God Who not only put it all together but also has all things under control. It's also more comforting."

"Hmmm. I didn't say I didn't believe in God," she said. "I just have a lot of questions."

"Questions are good, Barb, if you ask them with a mind open enough to allow God to answer them in His time and in His way. You, your group, and I are all going to Germany. In Germany this time of year, we're likely to see and hear a small bird known as the lesser whitethroat warbler. This tiny bird summers in Germany, nesting and raising their chicks. Come fall, the parent warblers head off to Africa for the winter, leaving their chicks behind. About two weeks later, the chicks head for Africa, too. Now I ask you, how do those little chicks find their parents in Africa without a loving God to direct their paths? By chance?"

"Wow! I never knew," Barb exclaimed.

"There are millions of arrows in God's creation quiver that point directly to Him. God's Word, the Holy Bible, from beginning to end, points to the promised Messiah, Jesus Christ. You see, Barb, there are no accidents. Nothing is by chance. Even our meeting was prearranged by a loving God so that you and I could have this conversation. He loves you and wants you to know and love Him."

"You've given me a lot to think about, Paul, but can we talk about something else for a while?"

"Sure, what would you like to talk about?"

"Well, let's talk about our families. Is your wife already in Germany, or is she meeting you in New York?"

"I'm a widower. My wife, Leah, died six years ago. The only family I have now is Rachel, my daughter; her husband, Jacob; and my twin grandbabies, Josie and Benjamin."

"I'm so sorry, Paul. I know what it is to lose a spouse. I'm a widow as well."

Just then, the stewardess arrived and said, "We'll be serving dinner soon. Senator, do you want the chicken or beef?"

CHAPTER 17
NEW YORK

As the "Connie" touched down in New York, Paul and Barb were still talking about everything imaginable. Neither of them seemed to run out of something to say about any subject served up. To an outside observer, it would appear that they were fond of one another.

"I've been to New York many times, and as a U.S. senator, I can get our little group into places most tourists can't go," Paul was saying. "So, what do you say? I'll just rearrange my flight schedule and leave for Germany tomorrow night with you and the girls. Besides, I really don't think we've talked ourselves out yet, and I know places and people here."

"That would be nice, Paul, but please don't inconvenience yourself on our account."

"It's no inconvenience, Barb. We're all staying at the Ritz. I'll arrange for all our luggage to be taken to the airport in the morning by the concierge, whom I know well and all we'll have to do is get ourselves to the airport before the flight leaves tomorrow evening."

"Okay, you've talked me into it," she said. "Let's get together tomorrow morning at the hotel to make our plans. I'm too tired tonight to think about what we'll do tomorrow."

The first-class passengers deplaned before the others, and Paul and Barb waited for the girls and little Eric just inside the terminal. Eric appeared to be asleep on Julie's chest with his head on her shoulder, but Julie and Cathy were still chatting excitedly about their ongoing adventure.

"Paul!" Julie exclaimed, looking first at him and then at her mother standing next to him.

"That's *Senator* Paul to you, little girl," Barb corrected. "Paul and I have plans about tomorrow's adventure that I think you'll both like. He's also staying at our hotel and knows people here who will make our visit more memorable. The hotel has already sent a vehicle to pick us all up. We'll go get some rest and regroup in the morning."

Next morning, everyone, including little Eric, slept later than usual. Barb's room phone rang at 9:14 a.m., according to the clock on the nightstand. She wasn't really asleep, just somewhere between asleep and awake. She picked up the phone, hoping it would be Paul.

"Hello," she said.

"Barb, this is Paul. Can you have your group ready by noon?"

"I think so. Maybe earlier."

"Good," he said. "We're going to start with the Statue of Liberty because that sight can sometimes be a lengthy wait. Then we'll visit the Empire State Building, followed by a drive down Broadway to see what plays are in production. After that, we'll just see how much time we have left before we have to catch our plane to Paris. We might be able to sneak one more sight into our agenda."

"Paul, you're so kind. I—we—appreciate what you're doing for us."

"Not a problem at all. I want you all to have a great trip. Glad to help. See you at noon."

Barb returned the phone to its receiver and yelled, "Get up, everyone! Paul wants us getting together at noon. Chop, Chop." And the panic-mode scramble was on for everyone to be ready to meet Paul by noon.

The phone rang again, and Julie answered. "Mom, it's Paul for you."

Barb took the phone. "Change of plans, Paul?" she asked.

"No change of plans—I just forgot to tell you all to have your luggage outside your hotel room by 11:30 for the concierge to pick up. Our luggage will already be checked onto the flight before we even get there."

"How do you do that?"

"There are ways," was all he said.

The exhausted group of five arrived at Idlewild forty minutes before their flight was scheduled to leave. Paul's attempted joke, "Is anyone tired yet?" was met with loud groans.

"Wall Street wasn't anything like I imagined," Cathy observed.

"But Chinatown was cute," Julie said.

"The good news," Paul said trying to lighten everyone's fatigue, "is that our flight to Paris will be about nine hours of rest."

"Nine hours? I thought it took longer than that to get to Europe, didn't you, Cath?" asked Julie.

"Yes, I did! Why is this flight shorter?"

"Because we're going by jet," Paul informed them. "We'll be taking the new Boeing 707. It'll cut hours off the trip. Now, I need to go to the Pan Am ticket counter for a few minutes. I'll be back shortly."

Barb, Julie, and Cathy chatted about their eventful day, appreciating the things Paul had arranged for them to experience beyond what Barb had envisioned for their New York visit. Paul returned in less than five minutes with a hand full of baggage claim tickets. "Here, Barb, these baggage claim checks are for you and the girls."

Barb shook her head slowly. "I don't know how you get these things done the way you do, Paul. It amazes me."

"Experience," was all he said.

They all hurried to their gate, presented their tickets and passports, and went to waiting area chairs and collapsed for the few minutes remaining before their flight.

When the flight was called, Paul got up and said, "Are you coming, Barb?"

"We'll have time to visit after I help Julie get Eric on the plane and settled." She smiled.

Paul nodded and went on.

Julie was shocked. She'd never seen her mom be this attentive to her and her son before. "Don't you like Paul, Mom?"

Barb looked at her daughter and smiled. It was the warmest smile Julie had ever seen from her mother. "Paul is the kindest, most interesting man I've ever met. Like you and Cathy, he's a Christian; and I admire his faith and knowledge of the God you three seem to know and love. I want to get to know Paul better, but I also want to get to know you and little Eric better. I definitely want to get to know this Jesus you three are always talking about better. You're different since you've been a Christian, Julie. I like what I see in you. I like what I see in Cathy. I like what I see in Paul. Maybe, in time, you'll start to like what you see in me."

Julie started crying. "Oh, Mom. I love you. What you just said makes me so happy."

——————————————— .✦. ——

Barb was dreading the end of their last flight into Stuttgart. Landing there would very likely end her encounter with Paul. There was only about an hour left until their arrival, and that made her very sad. She liked Paul . . . a lot. But she didn't know how to keep the thing going. She thought briefly about saying a prayer, but she didn't know how to pray and didn't know if the God she had avoided since her grandfather died would even listen to her.

Well, she thought to herself, *I have nothing to lose. God,* she prayed silently, *I like Paul. He is the most interesting man I ever met. Thank You for arranging for us to meet. Paul said You arranged it, and I like to think You did. I'd like to know him better and not lose touch with him. Amen.*

"Barbara," Paul said just as she finished her prayer, "I'd like to know if you'd be offended if I didn't call you Barb anymore. You see, in my mind, 'Barb' is a sharp, pointed object capable of causing pain. I can't see you as a 'Barb' because I don't see you in the way I just described."

Barbara looked at Paul and smiled. No one had called her "Barbara" since her grandfather had passed away. He always called her "Barbara June."

"Well, if you'd rather, my middle name is June," she said, hoping he'd take the hint.

"Barbara June," he said softly and slowly. "That is one classy and sophisticated name. I like it. I'll call you Barbara June, if you don't mind."

"Mind? I'd *love* it," she said and launched into the story about her grandfather's use of that name when she was a child. Her grandfather was a kind and thoughtful man who was a regular church-goer and lived what he believed.

Barbara June prayed again, *Thank You, God. He wouldn't be concerned about my name unless he had some thought in his mind about staying in touch. Thank You, thank You, thank You. Amen.* Maybe God *did* hear and answer her prayer. Maybe what Paul was telling her about God and Jesus was true. She had to know more.

"Paul," she said, "in the time we have left before we get to Stuttgart, I'd like for you to tell me about Jesus and how I can have the faith you and my daughter have."

"Praise the Lord," Paul said. "I've been praying for you during this whole trip, Barbara June. I'd like to continue getting to know you."

"It all seems so difficult," she said.

"God loves you. He wants you to love Him back. And that's not difficult. He wants to hear from you, Barbara June. Prayers don't have to be fancy or long. Just tell Him what's on your mind, good or bad. He can take either one, so don't sugarcoat anything. Just talk to Him like you would a friend."

For the first time in a very long time, Barbara June began to cry softly. Paul told her about Jesus, and Barbara June listened. And thousands of feet in the clouds over France, she surrendered her heart and life to Jesus Christ while she and Paul prayed together.

CHAPTER 18
THE SENATOR ARRIVES

The chaplain answered his ringing desk phone. "Chaplain speaking."

"This is General Short, Chaplain." Jacob didn't think he sounded too happy. "I thought you told me that you were not going to involve your father-in-law in our little disagreement about Ben's baptism," the general continued.

Jacob was speechless. He hadn't told the senator anything about it. "I didn't involve him, General. What gives you the idea that I did?"

"Because the senator just phoned me from the Stuttgart airport wanting a ride for himself and four others to this base. What's going on here, Chaplain? Is he bringing a Congressional delegation to check out me and my command? I can assure you, Chaplain, I'm *not* pleased."

"Honestly, General Short, I had no idea he was coming. I don't know anything about it."

"Don't lie to me, Chaplain."

"I'm not in the habit of lying to *anyone*, General Short, least of all my commanding general."

"For your sake, I hope you're not." The general ended the call.

Cal came into the chaplain's office with a puzzled look on his face. "What was that all about, Chaplain?"

"Apparently, my father-in-law has arrived. I'd better call Rachel and find out if she knows anything about this. General Short is blowing fuses."

Jacob picked up his phone, which was still glowing from the embers left by General Short's call, and phoned his wife. When she answered, he said, "Do you know if Laban is supposed to come for a visit?"

She was quiet for a couple of seconds before saying, "Why? Is he here?"

"Seems so. General Short just informed me that he's at the airport with four other people wanting a lift to the base, and he's accused me of throwing him into the deep end. What gives?"

"Oh, no! His coming was supposed to be a surprise for you when you use the baptismal pool for the first time—you know, since it was sort of his 'baby.'"

Jacob was quiet for a minute before he responded. "That's sweet, Rachel, but it's created a real hornet's nest for me. There are other issues you don't know about, and it's gotten real sticky all of a sudden. I have some damage control to conduct. We'll talk later, sweetie. Bye."

Jacob sat at his desk for a minute or two pondering what he should do next.

Cal was still standing in the Chaplain's doorway. "What now, sir?"

"I'm not sure, Cal. I don't quite know how to handle this one. The general thinks I sabotaged him, and it's put me in a real corner."

"My nana always told me that if I didn't know what to do next, the next thing I should do is get on my knees and pray to the One Who knows the answer."

Jacob rose from his desk and said, "And, as usual, your nana is right, Cal."

He walked to the front of the chapel and got on his knees. After about twenty minutes of prayer, he got up and went to Cal's office. "I'm going to the stockade to see a prisoner, Cal. I don't know how long I'll be." And he left.

Jacob decided to walk to the stockade. He wanted time to think over these recent events. He was feeling a sense of dread at having himself thrust into an awkward position with his commanding general. General Short had never been anything but cordial to him before, so this scenario was foreign to him. There was a reality here that he couldn't quite wrap his head around. What in the world was really going on?

Jacob decided that he should visit with Ben. Maybe Ben would have some answers for him. Besides, he needed to tell him that it didn't look like they were going to be able to go through with their plan to baptize him on Sunday, after all.

When Jacob arrived at the stockade, he entered and told the desk sergeant that he wanted to see Ben.

"I'm sorry, sir," the sergeant said. "That's not possible."

"Why not?"

"Because Ben Harkrider was found dead in his cell this morning. He apparently hanged himself."

"What? How? Why?" The questions spilled out of the chaplain. It didn't make any sense.

"I can't answer any of your questions, sir. You'll have to discuss any questions you have with Army CID."

As he left the stockade, his sense of dread was looming even larger than it had before he arrived. He knew now what he had to do. He ran back to the chapel and went to his office to phone Rachel.

She answered, "Hello?"

"Sweetie, get the babies ready to go over to Eric's apartment. I don't have time to explain right now; just do it. I'll be there in a few minutes to pick you all up." He left again, ran to his car, and hurried to their on-base residence to pick up Rachel and the twins. They weren't quite ready to go.

"Can you pack the diaper bags, Jacob?"

He put several cloth diapers in both bags, put a couple of clean baby bottles and nipples in each bag, and thought his chore done. He wanted to get moving . . . and fast.   He had no idea what evil was lurking or where it was coming from, but he was sure there was something out there that was beyond his control and could harm those he loved.

He put both bags over his shoulder and said, "Let's go!"

Rachel said, "You take Benjamin, and I'll carry Josie."

Fearing evil closing in, Jacob hurried his family out the door and quickly helped to get the babies and his wife into the car. Getting behind the wheel, Jacob drove very slowly through the base and got past the sentry at the gate before he picked up speed heading toward the apartment.

"What's going on, Jacob?   I don't think I've ever seen you this flustered."

"I don't know what it means, but Ben Harkrider was found dead in his stockade cell this morning. They told me he'd hanged himself. I have a *very* uneasy feeling about the whole thing. It makes absolutely no sense."

"Didn't you tell me he wanted to be baptized? Didn't he give his life to Christ?"

"Yes, and that's why none of this makes any sense to me. It doesn't add up."

They were both quiet for a few minutes until Jacob heard Rachel crying softly. "That's just so sad," she said. "I wonder why he did that?"

"I'm not so sure *he* did it—there's a very real possibility someone did it for him."

"But who would do that? And why?" Rachel asked as they arrived at the apartment.

"Who indeed?" Jacob replied. "Only someone who had a lot to lose because Ben Harkrider knew too much."

After Paul put the pay phone back on its hook, he had an uneasy feeling about the brief conversation he'd just had with General Short. He couldn't put his finger on it, but something was not right. Was it his imagination, or did the general sound paranoid?

He walked back to Barbara June and the girls. "There's an army car coming to take you all to the chapel on base. I need to rent a car and take care of some government business before I join you later."

"What's wrong, Paul?" Barbara June asked, puzzled.

"I'm not sure. There's something amiss here, and I think it needs my attention. The last time I was here, I uncovered a cancer that may not have been completely eliminated. I hope I'm wrong, but this thing has the appearance of being bigger than I first thought."

Paul made sure all their luggage was collected and had one of the German skycaps take it to the terminal entrance. He had the women follow the skycap outside, and leaving for the car rental agency, he told them he'd join them again in a few minutes. He got his rental and returned to the ladies at the terminal entrance and waited for the army staff car to arrive.

"Why are we going to the chapel, Paul?" Julie asked.

"Because I don't know where your apartment is and my son-in-law does. I do know it's not far off base, but I don't know exactly where it is."

Cathy and Julie were chatting excitedly as the staff car arrived to collect them. Paul went to the driver, introduced himself, and told the driver to follow his rental car to the base chapel. From there, he was to stand by for further instructions by the base chaplain.

The driver hesitated for a moment. "My instructions, sir, were only to pick you and four others from the airport and bring you all back to the base."

"Son," Paul said, "I am a United States senator. I am giving you new orders. If there are any problems resulting from this change in your orders, I will bear the burden, not you. Is that understood?"

"Yes, sir," the driver said.

"Fine. Now will you exit this vehicle and help load luggage so we can resume our trip, please?"

"Yes, sir," he said and got out of the staff car to open its trunk. The driver and Paul began loading luggage and then rearranged it to load more. The trunk wouldn't hold it all.

Paul went to his rental car and opened its trunk. "We'll put the rest in here. What won't fit, we can put in the back seat."

Once the car was loaded, the girls and little Eric got into the staff car's rear seat. "Barbara June," Paul said, "you can ride with me if you'd like."

She accepted Paul's invitation and got in his rental car, and they were off with the staff car in close pursuit into the ball of worms which constitute the streets of Stuttgart, Germany.

"I've been here several times, so I'm pretty familiar with the route to the post," Paul said. Barbara June nodded.

When the two-car parade arrived at the post's main gate, Paul stopped and showed the sentry his Senate I.D. and said, "The woman with me and the occupants of the staff car following me are all going to the chapel. I will be going to see General Short after they've been safely delivered."

The sentry saluted and said, "Yes, sir, Senator. The general notified us that you would be arriving and said to allow you to pass."

They proceeded past the gate and made the short trip from the gate to the chapel. Arriving at the chapel, Paul left his rental and, after telling the others to wait for a couple of minutes, went inside.

Inside the chapel, Paul went to Jacob's office; but the chaplain wasn't there. He turned to look for Cal, but he wasn't in his office either. The receptionist was also absent. Then he went into the chapel and found Cal redistributing hymnals to the pews.

"Hi, Cal," Paul said. "Do you know where my son-in-law is?"

"Yes, sir, Senator. We just heard you were here a little bit ago. He's gone to the stockade to see a prisoner. Left in one big hurry, too. He asked that you wait until he gets back."

"I'm afraid that won't be possible, Cal. I have other business to which I must attend. Do you know where Eric and Julie's apartment is located?"

"Yes, sir," Cal replied, "but I don't have a key to it."

"Who does?"

"Since the chaplain is at the stockade, the only other key is in Eric's hands."

"Can you take me to him?"

"Sure," Cal said. "Let me lock up, and we'll double-time to him."

As Cal locked the chapel door, Paul said to him, "I'll have the staff car follow us, and we'll go pick up Eric. Just take a seat in back of my rental car. We'll both go inside the motor pool and pry Eric loose for an hour or two. He still works in the motor pool, doesn't he?"

"Yes, sir, he does."

The two cars made their way slowly to the motor pool to get Eric because speed limits on military installations are low—and enforced. Arriving, Paul and Cal left the rental and went inside.

Cal introduced the senator to First Sergeant Tiller, the man in charge of the motor pool. "First Sergeant, this is Paul. He's a U.S. senator from Missouri, and we need for you to release Eric to us for a couple of hours."

The sergeant eyed Paul suspiciously for a long second before saying, "May I see some I.D., please?"

"Certainly, Sergeant. Will my U. S. Senate I.D. do?"

The sergeant studied Paul's I.D. for a second. "How do I know this is real?"

"You don't, Sergeant," Paul replied. "But because it is real and I have made an official request to you, if you deny my request, a substantial load of unpleasant things will soon descend upon you—things which, I can assure you, will not be enjoyable for you."

"Eric," Sergeant Tiller yelled. "Come here." Turning to Paul, the sergeant said, "I don't like threats."

Eric appeared from the front of a Jeep he was working on and said, "Yes, Sarge?" Then seeing Cal and the senator, he hurried over to where they were standing with his sergeant.

"Hi, Senator. How have you been?"

"I'm well, Eric. We need to borrow you for the rest of the day—with your sergeant's permission, of course." Paul winked at Eric. "And since it's Wednesday, maybe he'd even let you have tomorrow and Friday off as well, eh?"

"Sure," Eric said. "What do you say, Sarge?"

"Hey, I thought this was just going to be for a couple of hours. Now you want me to let him go for more than two days? You can't just walk in here and push me around," the sergeant argued, getting visibly steamed. "I'm in charge here."

"Sergeant," the senator said mildly, "you've insulted and impugned the character and official identification of a United States senator. Letting this man off for a couple of days is the least you can do to make amends."

"Okay, he can go, but you haven't heard the last of this, Eric."

"Cal and Eric," Paul said, "head on out to the car. I'll be along in a minute."

When they had left the building, Paul turned again to the sergeant and narrowed his eyes, looking straight into the sergeant's eyes. "If you don't like threats, Sergeant, perhaps you should behave in a less bullying manner. But you're wrong, Sergeant. Eric has, indeed, heard the last of this. It's you who hasn't. It's you who lacks understanding here. Do you read me?"

"There you go threatening me again," the sergeant said.

"Sergeant, I know full well how promotions in the military work. As a senator, I sit on promotion boards. Getting passed over repeatedly for promotion is a ticket to the exit. Do you still want to throw your weight around over something that doesn't really matter in the greater scheme of things and will very likely be forgotten by this time next week?"

The sergeant thought about it for a minute before answering, "No. Eric can take the rest of the week off, but I won't forget it by next week, Senator."

"Good decision, Sergeant. We'll consider this conversation concluded then, unless you decide you should do a bit of hazing later in retribution. Then we'll pick up this chat later, right here where we left off." Paul turned toward the exit to leave.

As Paul left the building, he saw Julie running toward her husband. Seeing her, Eric began running toward her. When they met, they embraced. Julie began kissing his face all over and finally planted a long kiss firmly on his lips.

Cathy got out of the staff car to watch Julie's reunion with Eric. Cal stopped in his tracks when he saw Cathy. He stood motionless until Paul caught up with him.

"Is anything wrong, Cal?" Paul asked.

"Who is that beautiful girl?" Cal asked, almost in a whisper.

"Her name is Cathy. She's Julie's best buddy. Kind of like you and Eric. Cathy's the one who led Julie to Jesus, Cal."

"Wow," was all Cal could whisper.

"Come on, Cal. I'll introduce you to her."

They moved past Julie and Eric, still wrapped in each other's arms.

"Cathy, this is Cal, Eric's buddy. Cal led Eric to Jesus just like you led Julie."

"Oh! Wow!" Cathy exclaimed. "I didn't know Eric had been saved. Jules and I were worried about how that piece of information was going to play out. Problem solved. Wonderful news!"

"Uh huh," was all Cal could manage to squeeze out.

"Julie, Eric, come on. Get in the car," Paul said. "We've got to get you to the apartment, so I can take care of some other business I need to address.

First Sergeant Tiller was livid when Paul left the motor pool. The motor pool was Tiller's turf, and he didn't want any snooty senator sticking an unwelcome nose in his business. Tiller had too much to lose to let this thing go. He and Horrible Harkrider had made a fortune during the Korean conflict in their shady dealings. It was Horrible Harkrider and Killer Tiller, the terrible twosome that made the shady world of the black market in Korea go round. Then Ben got himself discovered. As far as Killer Tiller was concerned, that just wouldn't do. Ben knew too much. And Ben had too many enemies—enemies in convenient places who would be more than happy to make a hanging look like a suicide for the right price.

Tiller went to his desk and opened the bottom drawer, taking a locked metal box out and unlocking it. He found two owl head .38 revolvers and removed one, checked to see that it was loaded, and put it in his pocket. He locked the box again and replaced the box in his bottom drawer again. He turned the pistol in his hand, admiring it.

Nice little weapon, this, he thought. *No one will ever know, since these little babies are not traceable.* It was time to pay a visit to General Short's meddling aide, Major Wells. Tiller was certain that it was the major who got Ben Harkrider arrested. He'd been nosing around in Ben's business for some time. He wasn't even subtle about it. *Time to pay the price for your snooping, Major.*

First Sergeant Tiller walked to General Short's headquarters building like he was just taking a Sunday stroll. *Nice day for a stroll,* he thought. It might even work out that the busybody senator could get caught in the crosshairs, too. Tiller smiled. That would be a nice bonus.

CHAPTER 19
APARTMENT MOVE IN

Jacob and Rachel had just gotten the twins out of their car when Paul's group arrived. Jules and Cath both jumped out of their cars at the same time and made a beeline toward Jacob's car and the twins, both of them wanting to hold one of the babies even before introductions took place. Rachel laughed and handed Josie to Julie, and Jacob handed Benjamin to Cathy. Holding babies just takes priority over everything.

Paul approached Jacob and said, "We need to talk."

"Indeed, we do," Jacob said. "But first, let's get everyone settled here."

The driver of the army staff car opened the car's trunk, and luggage was drawn out. Cal took one suitcase in each hand, Eric taking one to leave a free hand to open the apartment door with his key. Paul took two; Jacob took two; Barbara June took one and little Eric's hand in her other hand; and the staff car driver took the last two. The luggage-toting queue marched toward the door of the apartment with Eric leading the way. Julie and Cathy followed everyone else, each goo-gooing at the twins as they slowly brought up the rear. Apparently, the twins understood the language spoken by the girls because both babies were cooing back.

As Julie and Cathy entered the apartment, they found everyone standing patiently next to the burdens they had carried in, awaiting further instructions.

Julie said, "Oh," as if returning from another world and handed Josie back to Rachel. "Eric, which is our room?"

Eric gave her a quick tour of the apartment and told her which rooms he thought each of them would occupy. Julie agreed and began directing luggage traffic to the appropriate rooms. Once the luggage had been distributed, Paul dismissed the staff car driver, thanking him for his help. Then the senator turned to Jacob and motioned that they should go outside.

Jacob nodded and announced, "Paul and I have to return to the post and attend to some pressing business. We'll join you all later." Paul and Jacob left the apartment. When they were outside, Jacob said, "Let's take my car because it already has the proper base stickers, and we probably won't even have to stop at the gate."

Paul nodded agreement, and they walked to Jacob's car in silence. Once inside the car, Paul said, "There's something really smelly going on here. I'm not quite sure what to make of it. I have a hunch that Colonel Harkrider was just the tip of the iceberg."

Jacob nodded. "What you probably don't know is what I only discovered this morning shortly after you arrived. Ben Harkrider was found dead this morning in his cell. I was told it was a suicide by hanging, but I'm not buying it. I've been visiting him regularly to discuss his eternal destination. He had made a decision to accept Jesus Christ and wanted to be baptized. I've been badgering General Short to allow his baptism, but General Short has been dodging the issue, quoting 'security concerns.' So, I agree with you,

Paul; Ben Harkrider is only a very small tip to a very large iceberg. Ben knew too much for the rest of that iceberg to let him testify against them."

"What do you think we should do, Jacob? Our immediate resources are fairly limited. Neither of us know who is trustworthy and who is suspect."

"You're absolutely right, Paul; but we both know Who is *absolutely* trustworthy and will show us what avenues we should pursue, so we need to start there. Let's pray."

"I agree, Jacob. I'll start. Mighty and awesome Father, The Great I Am, El Shaddai, El Roi, the God Who hears us. We praise You and we seek Your wisdom in an area where we have no wisdom. It says in Your Word that when two or more are gathered in Your name, that You are with us.[7] We welcome You and thank You for honoring us with Your presence. We are faced with a situation that includes not only black-market thievery but now also includes the apparent murder of one of Your children. Your Word tells us that You will direct our paths, and we ask for that guidance now as we try to make sense of the things going on around us and to keep us and our loved ones out of harm's way as we seek truth in this matter. We lay this at the foot of your throne. Guide us, please."

"And, Lord, Abba Father, our heavenly Avi," Jacob added, "anoint us afresh with Your Holy Spirit to discern truth from lie and add to us the knowledge of who is trustworthy and who is not and who is guilty and who is innocent in this matter. We petition You in the name of Jesus Christ, Messiah, Yeshua, our beloved Savior and King. Amen."

---

7   Matthew 18:20

When finished, they looked at one another and said "Army CID," simultaneously. Jacob started his car, and he and Paul headed toward the office of Army Criminal Investigation Division.

"I picked up Rachel and the twins and brought them here because I'm not sure what we're up against, and I don't know to what lengths they'll go to protect their crimes," Jacob explained.

Paul nodded. "Good idea. It's best to be safe."

Jacob and Paul arrived at the building housing the CID and went inside. Paul showed his Senate ID to the staff sergeant at the reception desk and asked to see the officer in charge. The staff sergeant made a phone call, and a corporal appeared to escort them to the OIC's office.

"Please follow me," the corporal said.

They followed, and the corporal took them to a small reception area just outside the OIC's office where Captain Blaylock, Cal's former captain, was sitting.

Jacob and Paul looked at one another quickly, and then Paul said, "Captain Blaylock! Is everything all right with you?"

"Yes, sir, Senator. I'm fine. I'm just real uncomfortable with some of the things I see going on around here. Government property keeps disappearing with no trace. My own Jeep went AWOL this morning. I've been waiting for over an hour to see Lieutenant Colonel McChesney about it, but he's been too busy to see me."

"You can go in with us if you'd like," Paul said. "We may be here to discuss the same thing you want to talk about."

"That would be great."

Just then, the lieutenant colonel came out of his office to greet the senator. "Come in, Senator," he said, "It's nice to see you again."

Paul, Jacob and Captain Blaylock started toward the Colonel's office when the Colonel said, "Captain, I told you we'd deal with your Jeep later."

"He's with us, Colonel," Paul said.

Lieutenant Colonel McChesney looked puzzled but shrugged and said, "Okay. Come in."

When everyone was in the office, Jacob shut the door. "Do you know why we're here, Colonel?" Paul began.

"I imagine it has something to do with the last time we visited. Am I right?"

"Yes, you're right, but there's a new wrinkle with the death of Ben Harkrider."

"Terrible thing, that," Colonel McChesney said. "It kind of has me stumped. I didn't expect him to kill himself. Odd, isn't it?"

"It's even odder than you know, Colonel," Jacob added to the conversation. "You see, I've been visiting with Ben Harkrider ever since he was arrested. He had made a decision for Christ to come into his life and wanted to be baptized. Why would a guy want to end it when he'd made that decision?"

"With all due respect, Chaplain, Ben Harkrider may very well have been playing you like a cheap fiddle. A guy who's been involved in the stuff he's been up to might have been just stringing you along, playing the odds. Do you think that's possible?"

"Sure, it's possible," Jacob replied, "but I don't really think it's likely. I felt he was sincere."

"General Short phoned me and asked me what I thought of allowing Ben to be baptized," the Colonel said. "I told the general that I thought it was a bad idea."

"Just for the record, Colonel," Paul added to the mix, "how do you account for the fact that there are still reports of government property disappearing since Ben Harkrider's been out of circulation? Captain Blaylock's Jeep seemed to disappear just this morning. Ben Harkrider couldn't have been involved, since he died this morning. There's something rotten going on in Stuttgart."

"There is, indeed, Senator, but we're going to bring it to a screeching halt later this afternoon. And Captain Blaylock, you'll be getting your Jeep back tomorrow. I can't give you any more information than that, but we have the situation well in hand."

Jacob and Paul nodded, looking at each other.

"I didn't understand why General Short didn't want Ben to be baptized," Jacob said. "At least, I understand a little better now. It appeared to be vindictive on the general's part; but if you advised against it, it makes more sense now."

"Chaplain, you need to know that Ben was a well-known con man. We've been trying to nail him for his deeds for quite a while. He's had an 'under the radar' accomplice we just couldn't put a finger on. General Short and I decided to get Ben out of the way, putting him in the stockade, and see what floated to the surface. With Ben in the stockade, his accomplice overplayed his hand, and we will deal with him today. Case solved."

Paul got up from his seat and said, "Nice job, Colonel, I think we can rest easier now." He extended his right hand to shake the Colonel's hand.

"Thank you, Senator," he replied. "It's just part of the service."

Jacob and Captain Blaylock got up, each shaking the colonel's hand and thanking him. Captain Blaylock thanked Paul for once again coming to his rescue. Paul nodded, and he and Jacob walked to Jacob's car. Once they were seated, Paul looked at Jacob and asked, "So, what do you think, Jacob? Do you buy any of that?"

Jacob had a worried look on his face and answered, "I think it's too easy a solution. Things are being swept under the rug, and there are very likely people taking the fall for the misdeeds of others. Is that what you're thinking, too, Paul?"

"Bingo." Paul said. "And I think it's time we paid a visit to the general. But I think we should disguise our visit as a courtesy call to thank him for his efforts in getting the baptismal pool built. We can use that as a lead-in to what's happening in his command."

Jacob smiled and said, "Interesting approach, Paul."

Cal sat at the kitchen table, watching as Eric reconnected with his son by playing on the floor with him and his trucks. Julie, Cathy, and Barbara June all appeared from their bedrooms after dealing with their luggage contents and agreed to rearrange the furniture, first rearranging, then rearranging the rearrangement, and, still not happy, rearranging again. Big and little Eric had to move their truck operations four times during the process.

All the while, Cal kept his eyes on Cathy's movements, trying to be discreet but not succeeding too well.

When the ladies seemed satisfied with their efforts, Cathy turned to Cal and said, "What do you think, Cal?"

Cal shrugged his shoulders and said, "Furniture arrangement isn't my thing. I thought it was just fine the way it was when we got here." Cathy shook her head in disbelief.

"Did you know that Eric is going to be baptized this Sunday?" Cal announced, trying to change the direction of the conversation.

Julie's ears perked up and said, "Really, Eric? Are you getting baptized?"

Eric sat up, looked at his wife, and nodded.

"Can I get baptized, too?" Julie wondered aloud.

"I'd like to get baptized, too," Barbara June added.

"I'm sure the chaplain wouldn't mind. We have a new baptismal pool that's never been used before. We're already going to baptize Eric and another man this Sunday. I don't see any reason why we can't add two more," Cal said.

"That's just too wonderful," Barbara June exclaimed, beaming. "Mother and daughter getting baptized on the same day, along with the daughter's husband!"

Rachel, who had been sitting quietly in a corner feeding the twins added to the mix, "If Jacob has a problem with it, which I can't imagine he would, I'll convince him to change his mind. I'll just cry. He just can't stand for me to cry." She giggled. "And, Cal, don't you ever squeal on me about this."

"No, ma'am. I wouldn't dream of it. Cross my heart." Cal place an "x" over his heart with his right index finger.

Eric got up from the floor and announced, "I'm going to make a pot of coffee. Does anyone else want some?"

"I was hoping someone would make some," Cal said. "It just wasn't polite for me to ask."

Cathy came to the table and sat across from Cal and said, "Whew. Moving furniture is a chore."

Cal just nodded his agreement, before asking her, "How long are you staying here, Cathy?"

"I'm not planning to leave anytime soon. But I need to find a job once we get Julie and Eric settled in here. I may have a little bit of a problem with that since I don't speak any German. I don't suppose you have any ideas about job availability, do you?"

Cal's face broke into a huge smile. "As a matter of fact, I do. The receptionist we have at the chapel is leaving to go back to school in the States. Have you ever had a government job before? Do you type?"

"Yes, I type about fifty words per minute; plus, I worked at Warren Air Force Base in Cheyenne, Wyoming, before coming here."

"Sounds like the perfect solution to your problem and ours," Cal said. "I'll tell the chaplain, and I'm positive he can get it done. He's good about working things out."

Cathy smiled. "Will I get to work with you, Cal?"

His heart skipped a beat. "Yes," he managed to say above the butterflies he felt clamoring in his middle.

"I'd like that," she said as Julie joined them at the table.

"I have a question, Cal," Julie said. "Eric tells me you're knowledgeable about Bible stuff, so I want to hear about what you have to say about this rapture thing I've heard about. Do you really believe in it? Nothing like it has ever happened before, has it?"

"Let me first say, Julie," Cal replied, "that I believe that every word in the Holy Bible is true. The Holy Bible is God's love letter to all mankind. In the book of Genesis, chapter five, verse twenty-four, it says, 'Enoch walked with God: and he was not; for God took him.' To me, that sounds like he was raptured out of the world. Also, when

Jesus ascended after His resurrection, in front of many witnesses, He was lifted into Heaven. That sounds like a rapture to me, too."

"Interesting," Cathy said. "I'd never thought about those things in that light, but it certainly makes sense. I guess raptures may have happened before."

"As far as the rapture of the Church is concerned, there's widespread disagreement as to when, or even if, it's going to take place. My beliefs are based on what God's Word says in Revelation chapters eighteen and nineteen. In chapter eighteen, it tells the story of the fall of 'Mystery Babylon,' which I take to be the sinful secular world. Verse four says, 'And I heard another voice from heaven saying, *'Come out of her, my people, that ye be not partakers of her sins, and that ye receive not of her plagues.'* The quote 'come out of her, my people' isn't a suggestion; it's a command. Just like when Jesus raised Lazarus from the dead, His words were, 'Lazarus, come forth,' and that wasn't a suggestion either. It was a command. The Lazarus story is from the Gospel according to John, chapter eleven."

"That doesn't say anything about rapture, though, Cal," Julie said.

"That's true because the word 'rapture' isn't ever used in the Bible. But there's more. Chapter eighteen also talks about the bridegroom and His bride. Jesus is the bridegroom, and the Church is His bride. Chapter eighteen, verse twenty-three says, 'And the voice of the bridegroom and of the bride shall be heard no more at all in thee,' talking about the church on earth. When you add chapter nineteen, verse seven to the mix, it's all tied together: 'Let us be glad and rejoice, and give honor to him: for the marriage of the Lamb is come, and his wife hath made herself ready.' There can't be a wedding feast of the Lamb without the Church being in attendance, and the Church can't be in attendance if the Church is still on earth.

"So, to answer your question, Julie, yes, I do believe that the rapture will happen; and it could happen at any minute. My nana says the wedding feast of the Lamb is gonna' be one special wingding! In First Thessalonians, chapter four, verses sixteen and seventeen, the apostle Paul paints a picture of the rapture event for us when he says, 'For the Lord Himself shall descend from heaven with a shout, with the voice of the archangel, and with the trump of God: and the dead in Christ shall rise first: then we which are alive and remain shall be caught up together with them in the clouds, to meet the Lord in the air: and so shall we ever be with the Lord.' In 1 Corinthians 15:52, Paul says the rapture will happen in 'the twinkling of an eye,' so we need to be ready all the time. That pretty much settles it in my mind."

"I have a question, too, Cal," Barbara June said, joining the group. "I'm having trouble wrapping my head around the 'God in three persons' thing. I just don't understand how that's possible."

Cal nodded his head. "I have to admit that I had a problem with that at first, too. And it wasn't until my girlfriend back home wrote and told me that she was marrying someone else that I came to understand it better. That was a really dark time of faith-testing for me. I got to know and respect the chaplain during that time. He got me a pass to help me get my head together. I had several days alone in a hotel room to pray and read my Bible and pray some more and read my Bible some more.

"I read in Genesis chapter one during that time that when God created man, He said, 'Let *us* create man in *our* image.' I'd read that passage many times before, but it wasn't until I was on my knees in that hotel room that I finally saw the truth of what it said. 'Our' is a plural pronoun, indicating more than one owner. We humans have a body, a soul, and a spirit. There are three pieces to our being, and we don't even think about it. We just accept it. Since we come in three pieces, it shouldn't be too difficult to attribute three pieces to one God. Don't you think?"

"Oh, Cal! I'm so sorry you lost someone so special to you," Cathy said softly.

"Thank you, Cathy, but it's okay. I wrestled with God for three days about it, and He asked me, 'Cal, do you trust Me?' I said, 'Yes, Lord.' And then He said, 'Do you know I love you?' And I said, 'Yes, Lord.' And He said, 'I have a better plan for you.'"

"Wow, Cal," Cathy said. "I really like your relationship with Jesus. We need to talk some more. And I'd like to know more about your nana, too. She sounds like a neat lady."

Cal smiled broadly. "She is. We can all have a close relationship with Jesus if we read His Word and pray daily. Nobody can have a close relationship with Him without reading His Word and prayer on a daily basis. If we really want to be close to Him, we'll find the time to do it."

CHAPTER 20
THE PLOT THICKENS

When Paul and Jacob arrived at General Short's headquarters, there were two army ambulances parked in the circle drive and numerous MP's surrounding the building.

Paul looked at Jacob and exclaimed, "This isn't good! I wonder what's going on?"

"This is exactly the reason I picked up Rachel and the twins when I learned about Ben Harkrider. This thing is stinking more by the second, and I have bad feelings about all of it. Let's check with one of the MPs to see if they'll tell us anything."

Both men stepped out of the car and approached the nearest MP.

Paul announced, "We're here to see General Short, Sergeant. Can we get through?"

"No, sir. This building is under lockdown until further notice."

Paul produced his identification and showed the MP. "I'm a U.S. senator, Sergeant. I want to pass."

"With all due respect, Senator, there have been two people shot here," the MP replied. "For your safety, sir, would you please vacate the area until we're certain it's secure?"

"Yes, Sergeant, we'll leave; but before we go, can you tell me who's been shot?"

"No, sir," the sergeant replied. "I'm not cleared to release any of that information."

Paul nodded, and he and Jacob returned to the car.

"Jacob," Paul said when they'd settled into their seats, "I think we may be stirring up a hornet's nest by our activities, and we may be in this thing way over our heads. Whoever is behind this mess is willing to eliminate anyone perceived to be a threat, including you and me. And since neither of us know who can be trusted here and who can't be, we need to back way off."

Jacob thought about that for a minute before he agreed. "It has been kind of exciting, but I certainly don't want my wife and kids in harm's way."

"But I think there's one more thing we can do before we slam the door on this," Paul said. "I'm going to go to communications and make a radio telephone call to the president. Ike probably knows— or, at least, knows of—some of the players in this thing, and he can make things happen here that you and I can't."

"Sounds good, Paul," Jacob agreed. "I'll drive us across town to the communications center at Patch Barracks."

As they arrived back at Eric and Julie's apartment after Paul's phone conversation with the president and a very quiet trip back, Paul said, "I think we need to keep a lid on the events of the day until we're sure what's really going on. None of the others here need to know anything about what we've encountered today or any potential danger. What do you think, Jacob?"

"I agree, Paul, but you haven't filled me in yet on what the president said."

"I can't, Jacob. There's more here than any of us knew, and the president was aware of things headed south here. He's just going to expedite what his plans had been." Paul furrowed his brow suddenly. "You know, Jacob. It just dawned on me: if we hadn't gone to Lieutenant Colonel McChesney's office first, you and I might have gotten in the middle of whatever was going on at General Short's headquarters today. We were delayed by God's grace, my brother."

"I think you may just be right, Paul," said Jacob. "We need to pause and give thanks for the Lord's protection."

Paul nodded in agreement, and both men bowed their heads in silent thanks.

They both exited the car and entered the apartment to find themselves outsiders to a lively conversation among their group of friends and relatives about baptism.

On seeing Paul, Barbara June jumped up and said, "Oh! Paul! Do you think it would be all right if Julie and I were baptized along with Eric and the other man this Sunday?"

Paul looked at Jacob and said, "It's your call, Chaplain. I think it's a wonderful idea, but it's up to you to decide."

Jacob smiled and said, "Of course. We may as well utilize the new baptismal pool to its fullest on its inaugural dunking."

"Well," Paul added, "what would you think if I wanted to baptize Barbara June myself?"

"Oh, Paul," Barbara June gushed, "That would be just splendid if you did."

"I guess that settles it, Paul," Jacob said, putting his endorsement on the plan. "You get to baptize Barbara June. And if no one has any objections, I'll baptize the rest."

"One more thing," Paul added. "I think we should do the baptisms at the end of the service. The last time I did a baptism—Jacob, that's when I baptized you—we did it first, and I nearly froze to death during the service. What say? Last?"

Jacob started laughing at the recollection. "Yes. I nearly froze, too, so that's a good idea."

Late Friday afternoon, the chaplain's telephone rang. "Hello, Chaplain speaking," he answered.

"Major, this is General Short; do you have a minute to speak with me?"

"Absolutely, General, how can I help you?"

"Well, first of all, I want to apologize to you for our last telephone conversation several days ago. There were strange goings-on that seemed totally out of control, and I wasn't sure where the grease needed to be applied. There seemed to be multiple squeaking wheels. Do you know what I mean?"

"Not entirely," Jacob said, "But there did seem to be oddities all about. The senator and I came to your headquarters to pay a visit; but MPs had the place surrounded, and we weren't allowed in."

"That must have been when First Sergeant Tiller made his final poor decision and paid for it with his life. We were making preparations to arrest him that afternoon for his misdeeds, but he hastened the process when he tried to get rid of my aide, Major Wells. What Tiller didn't know was that Major Wells was not who Tiller thought he was.

He was acting as my aide, but he was sent here specifically to get things stirred up, so we could figure out who all the bad guys were. We knew Harkrider was, for sure, but we didn't know that Tiller was in this thing, too."

"That certainly explains why First Sergeant Tiller was so disrespectful toward the senator," Jacob said. "His behavior toward Paul was borderline insubordinate."

"That sounds like Tiller," the general said. "He got too big for his britches. Appears to me, he thought he was above getting caught. We were able to snag several other minor players as well."

"You said two people were shot, General. Who was shot besides First Sergeant Tiller?"

"Well, the way it came down was when Tiller came into the building, he was detained at the reception desk to determine if he actually had business there. The desk sergeant had already been alerted to Tiller's imminent arrest. When Tiller's access to the building was denied, Tiller pulled a pistol from his pocket. I guess he decided to shoot his way in. Dumb move. He was apparently inept with firearms; and the weapon discharged, ricocheting off the floor and striking a second lieutenant coming down the stairs. The bullet hit the lieutenant in the left calf. He'll be okay. The desk sergeant pulled his .45 and shot Tiller once. Once, in this case, was enough. He died on the spot."

"I'll let Paul know what happened, General. We were wondering what all the commotion was about when we tried to visit you. And as far as apologizing to me goes, there's no need. I know you have a lot more on your mind than most people realize."

"Thank you, Major, but I wanted things proper between us."

"I appreciate that, General. By the way, we're having four baptisms this Sunday. You're cordially invited to attend. It is, after all, by your generosity that we have a baptismal pool."

Thank you, Major. My wife and I may do just that."

CHAPTER 21
JOY COMETH IN THE MORNING

Since it was the Saturday before the big day of the baptismal pool inauguration, Eric knew that Cal would be at the chapel making final preparations before the big day. Eric needed to talk with his best buddy. They'd become close, and for this, he needed Cal.

He opened the chapel doors and poked his head in to listen. No sound. He walked in and went to Cal's office. No Cal. He walked into the chapel and saw Cal in front, on his knees, obviously praying. Eric sat quietly on a back pew and waited. His heart was in turmoil. His stomach was, too. He felt sick. Julie had told him everything; and he felt angry, betrayed, and humiliated. She had cried through her whole confession; and when she was done, she had obviously expected him to say something. He didn't. He just got up, walked out of the apartment, and came here. He didn't know what else to do or where else to go but to see Cal.

After several minutes, Cal got up and came toward Eric. "I heard you come in, Eric, but I was kind of busy. What's up?"

"I don't know how to start, Cal. I'm hurting," Eric began. "I'm hurting like I think you were when you got that letter from your old girlfriend. I'm just heartsick, Cal."

"So . . . do you want to talk about it?"

"Yes—and no," Eric answered. "I really just want it to go away; but it's out now, and I know it can't go away. It's like seeing something you don't want to see. You can't un-see it. But oh, how it hurts."

Cal just remained silent. He knew Eric would open up eventually and tell him about what was bothering him, but he had a sense of what the problem was. And Cal was aware, too, just how much it did hurt.

"It's Julie," Eric said, telling Cal what he already suspected. Cal nodded. Eric started showing signs of tears. "She had a one-nighter, got pregnant, and had an abortion."

Cal watched silently as his friend mourned what he thought was his crumbling marriage, the pieces falling around him like volcano ash. "You may not think so now, Eric," Cal said after several quiet minutes, "but the fact that she told you at all shows that she trusts and loves you."

"For once, Cal, I think you're wrong," Eric said with venom in his voice. "Cheaters are *not* showing love, buddy!"

"Aren't you forgetting something, Eric? Didn't you have a cheating problem once? Did you tell Julie about it? The answers to those three questions, in order are yes, yes, and, probably, a loud no."

"That was different," Eric said defensively.

Cal chuckled. "You're lying to yourself, Eric. Your behavior was no different than hers. I'd be willing to bet that her actions were before she met Jesus. I know your actions were before you totally gave your life to Him. Now, let me ask you a question. Did Jesus pick and choose which sins you'd committed to forgive and which not to forgive?"

Eric didn't answer.

"I take your silence to mean that you're aware that He forgave all, no strings attached," Cal continued. "Now, don't you think you owe your wife the same courtesy? Remember what Jesus said in His Sermon on the Mount in Matthew 5 and 6. If we forgive the sins of others, God will forgive us, but if we don't forgive the sins of others, why should we expect God to forgive us? He won't."

Eric's face began to soften, and he looked Cal straight in the eye.

"A couple of other things Jesus said in the Sermon on the Mount are, 'Blessed are they that mourn: for they shall be comforted,' and 'Blessed are the merciful: for they shall obtain mercy.' You're mourning your wife and your marriage right now, buddy. Be merciful, and you'll receive mercy. I love you like a brother, Eric. And because I love you like a brother, I'm going to tell you the hardest thing for Christians to do—and that's for us forgive. In the Lord's Prayer, Jesus taught us to ask God to forgive us our sins just like we forgive the sins of others against us. My nana says when we don't forgive, it's just like we drink poison ourselves, hoping the other person will die. The other person isn't harmed at all—we are."

After several minutes of reflection, Eric said, "Cal, I could really use one of your wonderful prayers right now. Will you pray with me?"

Cal nodded, and they prayed together. When Cal whispered his amen, he said, "What we need to do now, my friend, is get together with Julie and Cathy, and the four of us put this problem in perspective. You, my friend, have to make your confession and apologies as well."

When Eric and Cal arrived at the apartment, they found Julie crying and saying, "I never should have come here. I never should have told him." While Cathy hugged and tried to comfort her.

"Let's all sit here at the table," Cal said. "Are we the only ones here?"

"Yes," Cathy answered. "Paul took Barbara June and little Eric over to Jacob and Rachel's place."

Cal nodded. "That's good. Now, let's all take a seat because Eric has some things to confess to Julie."

Julie stopped crying, looked at Cal, then Eric and said, "Things? How many things?"

Cal heaved a heavy sigh. "How about we all just sit and act like adults without letting our emotions fly away wildly? Remember what Jesus said: 'He that is without sin among you, let him first cast a stone.'"[8]

Cathy gave Cal a big smile, and she guided her friend to the table.

"Eric," Cal began after they were all seated, "I told you that Julie must love and trust you a lot to have confessed to you what happened while you were away."

Eric nodded. "Yes, you did."

You know yourself that being separated from those we love creates a loneliness that can only be described as desperate. It's a vacuum that we keep trying to fill when our loved ones are not with us."

Eric nodded.

"Then, what do you have to say to Julie?" Cal continued.

Eric looked at Cal with a clueless expression.

"Do you love her?" Cal asked.

"Yes," Eric said to Cal.

"Don't tell me, Eric. Tell *her*!"

Cathy wanted to giggle at Eric, but she was fascinated with Cal's skill. It was obvious to her that he had a future in pastoral counseling.

---

8   John 8:7

Eric fixed his eyes on the table in front of him and quietly said, "I love you, Julie."

"Eric, you're my best friend," Cal said. "So I have to tell you that if I were Julie and you expressed your love to me in that way, without looking at me, I wouldn't believe you. Can you look into the eyes of your lovely wife and express your love for her?"

Eric looked up from the table and looked into Julie's eyes. Tears were in her eyes. Eric began to tear as well. "Julie, I love you. I forgive you."

"I love you, too, Eric," Julie said. "And Cal was right when he said that I must trust and love you to confess what I had done. So my question to you is this: do you trust and love me enough to tell me what Cal says you need to tell me?"

Eric nodded his head and began the story.

When Eric had finished, Cal said, "Why don't you two get alone and finish this? It's personal between the two of you. It's your business from B.C.—before Christ. You belong to Him now. My suggestion is that you two go into your bedroom together, get on your knees together, and pray together. And tomorrow, you'll be baptized together."

Eric and Julie got up from the table, joined hands, and went into their bedroom, shutting the door.

Cathy looked at Cal. "You're something, mister. That could have gone off the tracks at several points, but you stayed the course. I'm impressed. I don't see you as a one-trick pony, so what other wonderful tricks do you have in your tool bag?"

CHAPTER 22
BAPTISM DAY

al anxiously awaited the arrival of Cathy and the others outside the chapel. It was a beautiful, sunny morning in Bavaria. This would be the first of what Cal hoped to be many more Sundays he and Cathy would spend together in church worshiping their Savior. The others arrived in two cars—the chaplain, Rachel, the twins, and Cathy in the chaplain's car and Paul, Barbara June, Julie, Eric, and little Eric in Paul's rental car. Cal met them at the chaplain's car as Cathy emerged carrying Josie.

Cathy smiled at Cal and said, "This baby is just the sweetest little bundle."

They all went inside the chapel and split into groups. Rachel, the twins, Cal, Cathy, and little Eric took seats in the chapel, and the baptism candidates took seats on the front row as "Big Smitty" arrived. Paul and Jacob took to the pulpit area. After taking their seats, Cathy slipped her hand into Cal's and smiled at him. Cal was elated, but he didn't think he could talk.

The chaplain began the service and the forty-or-so attendees sang, "How Great Thou Art." He then gave his sermon based on Jesus' parable of the prodigal son, tying it in with the upcoming baptisms. Then "Amazing Grace" was sung, and the baptisms began.

Since Paul had actually gotten the baptismal pool to happen, Jacob had thought it only proper that Paul baptize Barbara June first. Paul asked her, in front of those gathered, if she accepted the shed blood of Jesus Christ to atone for her sins and if she believed that her salvation was by grace alone. She answered yes to his questions, and he lowered her beneath the water.

Then Paul and Jacob traded places, and the event was repeated three more times with "Big Smitty," Julie, and Eric last.

After the baptismal service was concluded and the rest of the Sunday worshipers had left the chapel, the little group left was feeling spiritually exhilarated.

"I'm so excited, I could just jump and leap and praise the Lord," Julie exclaimed.

"You just quoted Scripture there, Julie," Cal said. "That's the way Scripture describes the events after Jesus healed the lame man."

"I feel the same way as you do, Julie," Chaplain Jacob said. "Our little group of believers is growing, and I want to hold on to today's events just a little longer. Why don't we do what we used to do at Pastor Phil's church in New York? Let's all go out to dinner for an afterglow. What do you think, Rachel? Do you think the babies will do okay?"

"I think they'll be fine. Where did you have in mind? We probably should go someplace where we can get a room to ourselves."

"I know a place just off post," submitted Cal. "It's a German restaurant that serves a wide range of German food—if you like kraut."

"The last time I was here, I had dinner at an Italian restaurant with General Short," said Paul. "I noticed that they had several private rooms . . . and I'm not too keen on kraut."

"A good Italian restaurant would certainly bring back some good memories, eh, Rachel?" asked the chaplain. "Let's do that, unless there are other suggestions."

Everyone agreed that Italian food would be best, and they loaded themselves into the chaplain's car and Paul's rental car with Paul saying to the chaplain, "I'll lead the way. It's about a mile from the gate."

The short "hallelujah parade" wound its way through the streets of Stuttgart to the restaurant. Once there, they piled back out of the two vehicles and headed inside. Paul took the lead and asked for the owner to explain that a private room was needed for their little gang. The owner didn't speak English. Paul didn't speak German or Italian. "Can any of you guys help me here?" Paul asked.

Cal stepped forward and said, "Zimmer," to the owner, who showed them to a private room ample for their needs.

"Good job, Cal," the chaplain said. "I didn't know you spoke German."

"I don't," Cal said smiling. "One of the very few words I know is zimmer. It means 'room.' Beyond that, I'm pretty useless in the German language."

"You had just the right word 'for such a time as this,'[9] my friend," Cathy said as she once again slipped her hand into Cal's.

"I can tell you and Julie are friends," Cal said, smiling. "She quoted the Gospels; and now you're quoting the book of Esther, one of my favorites in the Old Testament."

---

9   Esther 4:14

They all took their seats. Cathy sat next to Cal. Barbara June sat next to Paul. Julie sat next to Eric with little Eric sitting on his daddy's lap. Jacob sat next to Rachel with the twins next to her in child carriers and Smitty next to the babies. Menus were handed out; and to everyone's delight and relief, the food items on the menu were illustrated with pictures. Speaking German or Italian wasn't necessary. The diners only needed to point to the picture of the meal they wanted to enjoy.

After everyone's order was taken, Rachel turned to Paul. "Now that your baptismal pool has been launched, what are your plans, Dad? Are you going to run for a third term in the Senate, or are you going back to what you love most—preaching and teaching the Word of God?"

Paul was quiet for a moment before answering. "I'm actually able to do the Lord's work in the Senate. Opportunities to do His will arise on almost a daily basis; but at some point, I'll have to give it up. I believe in term limits for citizen servants of the government; and if I do run for a third term and win, it will be my last term. I won't run for a fourth." Paul looked at Barbara June. "Of course, there are times when the unforeseen grabs our hearts and gives us a good shaking. I was thinking of taking a few days to explore Paris on the way home. Assuming Barbara June is agreeable to that."

Barbara June turned and looked Paul straight in the eye. "I should say *not!*"

Paul stammered for a second before blurting, "Separate rooms, of course."

"Paul, I'm very fond of you, but you're asking me to accompany you to Paris, one of the most romantic cities in the world. Why would

I want to go to Paris with a man who has not even once tried to hold my hand?"

The never-at-a-loss-for-words Paul looked thunderstruck as the women in the group, always more astute in matters of the heart than men, giggled.

"And," Barbara June continued, "perhaps future invitations might be delivered in a less public setting. This type of thing doesn't necessitate the media being alerted."

"My dad is proof," Rachel said, "that sometimes men are clueless, Barbara June!"

AUTHOR'S NOTE

God's love is incredible. God's love is eternal and constant. God's love is uniquely expressed to each person He's created in ways that are as unique to each person as each person is unique to God's creation. And His love is expressed to each person through Jesus Christ. He knows what we need before we need it.

As one of God's unique children, I have never appreciated being preached at or lectured about anything. It appears to me that most other people whom I've known feel pretty much the same way. My observations tell me further, though, that people, including me, don't mind hearing a story. I'd like to share my own story with you.

As a twentyish man in the early 1970's, I was an anxious mess. My life seemed to be crumbling around me, and I was frantic about how to stop it from crumbling further. I was the father of three young children I adored and had a wife, who, as the nursery rhyme says, "he couldn't keep her."

Enter the person in my life who was my "Cal." He and I worked an evening shift together; and when our evening meal time arrived, he would find someplace to spend his meal break reading his Holy Bible as he ate. The other guys on our shift had long since quit razzing him about his lunchtime activities because he had made it perfectly clear that he wasn't bothered by it. I watched him over a period of several weeks as he wore his peacefulness like a garment of spring breezes. I didn't know what he had, but I wanted it. I hoped that the armor of his peace could shield me from the darkness pounding me at each turn. I finally asked him about it.

I didn't feel threatened by his "religious" activities because, after all, I'd been raised attending a church that told me all sorts of stories about Jesus. I pretty much knew all about Him. I could name the four Gospels. I still had a Bible that had been given to me as a teen by my mom and stepdad. I'd even picked that Bible up a few times and tried to read it. *Surely,* I reasoned, *I could handle anything he told me.* As important as what he told me was, it was what he *showed* me by his life about what was written in the Holy Bible that impressed me most.

- He showed me that Jesus is the light of the world and leads us out of darkness (John 8:12).
- He showed me that I, and every other person who ever has or will live, am guilty before a holy God of wrongdoing (Rom. 3:23.)
- He showed me that the penalty for my guilt before a holy God is death (Rom. 6:23).
- He showed me that I can never earn forgiveness by my efforts, because no matter how good I try to be, my "goodness" can never be seen by a holy God as anything more than "filthy rags" (Isa. 64:6).
- He showed me that Jesus is the Messiah God promised because of His love for all mankind (John 3:16, John 6:69).
- He showed me Jesus lived the only perfect life (Matt. 17:5).

- He showed me that Jesus' sacrifice by dying on a Roman cross as God's own Son at the Jewish feast of Passover and His resurrection three days later is the only remedy for sin and death—that remedy leading to salvation (Acts 4:10-12, Matt. 17:22-23).
- He showed me that Jesus is the only Path to God the Father (John 14:6).
- He showed me the commandment Jesus left for us to follow (Matt. 17:37-40, John 15:12, 17).
- He showed me how Jesus disciplines us for not following His commandments (Matt. 7:21-23, Rev. 3:5, 16).

After sharing with me the evidence that Jesus *is* Who the Holy Bible says He is, He asked me if I was ready to invite Jesus into my heart and life to be my Savior. I accepted; and he asked me if I believed that if I confessed my sins, God was "faithful and just to forgive [my] sins and cleanse me of all unrighteousness" like He promised in 1 John 1:9.

I said yes, and he led me in a prayer like the following: "Awesome Adonai, the Great I AM, El Shaddai, the mighty God, I approach your throne as a sinner who needs a Savior, a lost sheep who needs a Shepherd. I acknowledge that Yeshua Jesus is Your sinless Son, Who suffered on a Roman cross and sacrificed Himself in my place to make me acceptable to You. Sinless Yeshua paid for my many sins. It is by Your mercy and grace alone through the shed blood of Jesus that I make this plea. I ask for Your forgiveness in the name of Jesus, the new King of my heart. Amen."

Since that October evening in 1974, my life has never been the same. My friend told me to find a church that teaches God's Word and get involved in that church's ministries. He told me that an ember that is removed from the fire will soon go out. Christians who keep themselves from fellowship with other Christians will soon lose their fire as well. Once we are saved from sin and death, many want to retire, sit back, and do nothing more. But we're not called to do that. We're called to "love [our] neighbors as [ourselves]."[10] If our neighbor is hungry, we are to feed him; if he is thirsty, we are to give him drink.[11] If our neighbor is hurting, we are to comfort him.

Christianity is more than a religion. Religion is mankind trying to live by a set of man-made rules and conditions in order to appease a man-made god. Christianity is God Himself knowing that sinful mankind could *never* live up to His holy standards and providing *the only* way for the creation He loves to be reconciled to him: the sacrifice of Jesus Christ, God the Father's only Son. Christianity is a day-by-day, hour-by-hour relationship with Jesus. I recommend it highly!

---

10   Mark 12:31
11   Proverbs 25:21

ABOUT THE AUTHOR

Born in Kansas City, Missouri, in 1947, early "baby boomer" C. M. Needham, known as "Spark" to his friends, spent his growing up years in Doraville, Georgia, and Hurst, Texas, as well as Kansas City. After high school graduation in 1965, Spark headed to San Diego, California, for U. S. Navy boot camp and spent twenty-five years in the navy, active and reserve, retiring in 1999. From 1965 to 1999, he had ten years of broken service. His civilian jobs included personnel representative for a public utility and loan officer for a mortgage company.

In 1980, Ottawa University, in Ottawa, KS, awarded him BA degrees in business and English in 1980, and he continued his education at the University of Kansas MBA program.

Spark's first published work was "Dad's Birthday Surprise," a short story which appeared in *Capper's* (June, 2009), and the story was turned into a children's book titled, *My Dad's Birthday Surprise*, published by Ambassador International in 2014.

Spark has one grown son, three grown daughters, and one grown stepson. He and his wife, Jean Libby, whom he calls his "magic Jeannie," live in Sugar Creek, Missouri.

When Lena Neubauer is sent from Germany to America to help her immigrant brother on his farm and with his young children, she never expects what awaits her in antebellum America. With family honor and devotion propelling her across to an unknown world, Lena soon finds herself stepping into this strange world. After tragedy strikes, Lena finds herself finally at the crossroads and must make a decision that will affect her future—and her family's future—forever.

David al-Nassery is a man of renown. Hailing from distant Chaldea, he has made a name for himself in the United Kingdom as a philanthropist and an advocate for the political interests of the Middle East. Yet even as he surrounds himself with allies, enemies from his past await him. When confronted by a figure from his past on a cold, dark night, David is forced to reckon with the decisions he made in Chaldea—choices that cost thousands their lives.

Betty is sure that Ida Lou does not belong in their church when the woman shows up to the Good Friday service with her small dog in tow. But before she knows what's happening, Betty—along with the other women of the WUFHs (Women United For Him)—is pushed into helping the woman. God works in mysterious ways—and through ordinary people. The town of Prosper is about to experience some drama—and it all starts with a dog who comes to church.

www.ingramcontent.com/pod-product-compliance
Lightning Source LLC
Chambersburg PA
CBHW050021070726
47506CB00015B/759